"LOOK!"

A great tree spread in front of them, filling the whole width of the canyon with its boughs.

"Old Man of the Oak, hear me. My name is Geniolien Dolengwrydd. I've come all the way from Ranath Drallm to find you."

"Why...have...you come?" The sound of the tree resembled that of an old man laboring to push out words.

"To ask you to use your power, your earth magic, to bind the walls of Ranath Drallm and make them so that nothing, not even goblin fire power, can destroy them."

"Earth magic...can bind. For a price."

"All right," Geniolien said, "what do you want?"

"Magic," the tree boomed back, "or *life*."

A MagicQuest Book

The Princess and the Thorn

PAUL R. FISHER

TEMPO BOOKS, NEW YORK

MagicQuest Books by Paul R. Fisher

THE ASH STAFF
THE HAWKS OF FELLHEATH
THE PRINCESS AND THE THORN

This Tempo Book contains the complete
text of the original hardcover edition.
It has been completely reset in a typeface
designed for easy reading, and was printed
from new film.

THE PRINCESS AND THE THORN

A Tempo Book/published by arrangement with
Atheneum

PRINTING HISTORY
Atheneum edition/1980
Tempo edition/October 1984

ISBN: 0-441-67918-8

Tempo Books are published by The Berkley Publishing Group,
200 Madison Avenue, New York, New York 10016.
Tempo Books are registered in the United States Patent Office.
PRINTED IN THE UNITED STATES OF AMERICA

*For Meri and Cyneil
and for all those who have been Arien*

Son of Thorn
Through woods has passed
O'er tossing sea,
Through worlds grey,
And mountains green,
To reign at last
In seven seats at mouth of One
With snow-white walls, strong and fast,
Falling ne'er by binding spells
Brought by she from distant vales.

Gone with Goodblade
And robe unspun,
With Amreth's daughter,
With him of Sharicom.
Gone with music, lore, and wisdom.
Parted from him who yearns to go
Into the lands of ice and snow.
Doomed to mourn for him who falls
In battle at a kingdom's walls.

Contents

SAGA FIVE

SAGA SIX

The Descendants of Garren Mehridene

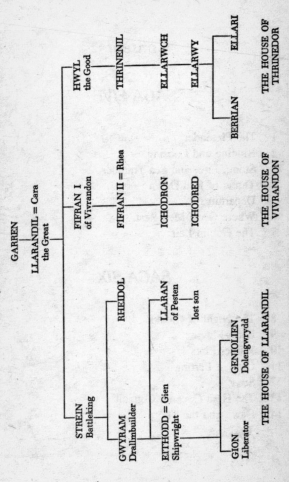

GARREN

LLARANDIL = Cara
the Great

STREIN
Battleking

RHEIDOL

FIFRAN I
of Vivrandon

HWYL
the Good

GWYRAM
Drallmbuilder

LLARAN
of Pesten

FIFRAN II = Rhea

THRINENIL

EITHODD = Gien
Shipwright

lost son

ICHODRON

ELLARWCH

GION
Liberator

GENIOLIEN
Dolengwrydd

ICHODRED

ELLARWY

BERRIAN

ELLARI

THE HOUSE OF LLARANDIL

THE HOUSE OF VIVRANDON

THE HOUSE OF THRINEDOR

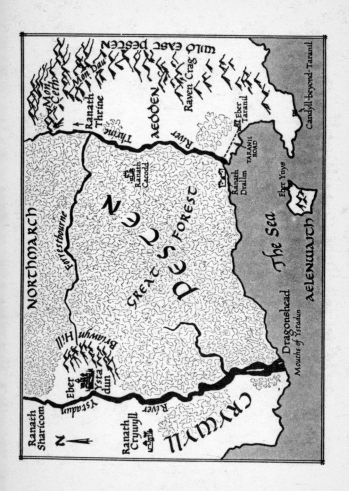

SAGA FIVE

· 1 ·

The Pretender

THROUGH THE GRILLWORK of the gate, Merani saw her arrow embedded in a tree trunk, quivering slightly.

She cursed under her breath. "Now I'll have to get a gardener to unlock the gate," she muttered. She had fired arrows into this garden before, and she knew the gate was always locked, for no one lived in the building beyond the trees. All the same, having to find a gardener was such a bother that Merani shook the gate furiously. To her surprise, the bolt clattered back, and the gate, with a squeal, yawned open.

Checking to see if she was being watched, Merani crept into the garden. When the shadows of the first trees fell across her, Merani heard water, probably from a fountain near the rosebushes by the north wall. A bee buzzed by her. Sunlight flashed across her face as she reached for her arrow. But as she tucked it under her arm, she heard a voice above the hum of the breeze in the trees.

"Is that your arrow?"

A woman appeared from behind a rosebush. Merani felt herself turning red, but she nodded. "I hope I didn't hurt anything," she said. "If I did, I'm sorry."

The woman smiled. "You haven't done any harm. Just frightened me a little!" She held up a finger for Merani to see; a drop of blood, round and glossy like a pearl, shone on her fingertip. "I was cutting roses when your arrow hit that tree. My finger snagged a thorn—"

3

"I'm sorry," Merani said. "I didn't mean to put an arrow in your tree or come into your garden without asking. I thought no one lived here."

"Nobody did until a few days ago," the woman said. She seemed younger now than when Merani had first seen her. "I must admit, I jumped when I heard the gate open. After that arrow, I thought we were under goblin attack. I was glad to find it was you."

Merani, turning to leave, suddenly noticed that the lady wore a brooch that displayed the golden sun of Pesten. The woman, no doubt, was one of the distant relatives of the High King.

"With your leave," Merani said, "I'd better go."

"You don't have to. At least not so soon."

Merani looked at her arrow. "I've trespassed enough already."

"I think," the woman said, placing green eyes on Merani, "that the trespassing rules apply more to the warriors—"

"But I am a warrior," Merani said. "I'm an archer."

"But you're also a young lady," the woman said, "and you're quite welcome in my garden now that I know you're not trying to shoot me. Stay as long as you like."

Stiffening, Merani glanced around her.

The woman turned back to the rosebush and cupped her hands under one of the blossoms. "What's your name?" she asked.

"It's Merani. Merani Felleira."

The woman nodded knowingly. "You're the former princess from Fellheath, aren't you?"

Merani looked at the nearest rose. "I wasn't exactly a princess—just sort of. Actually, I've always been more of an archer."

The woman tugged sharply at the rose stem, then drew the flower out of the bush and closed its stem in her hand. "I understand. I'm sort of a princess myself."

"I don't think I've seen you before," Merani said. "What's your name?" She glanced at the brooch, then added, "my lady."

At this the woman looked suddenly at her flower and remained silent for so long that Merani thought she hadn't heard the question. "My name," the woman said, turning the rose in her hands, "is Mira. That's short for Miralien, which is only for formal occasions. I don't like formal occasions, so please call me Mira. Do you like my garden?"

"Very much."

"It's a little overgrown," Mira said. "I've been away for too long. But I'll weed it well as summer goes on. If I can find time, that is."

"You could get the gardeners to weed it for you."

"I could," Mira said. "But I don't want to. This is my garden, after all. Here, let me show you around, then we'll go in and have something to eat."

"I really need to go back to the common to practice with my bow," Merani said. "And I don't want to trouble you."

Mira's dark eyebrows arched. "Trouble me? Nonsense. Do you see that flowerbed near the fountain? Do you recognize those flowers?"

"Fellblossoms!" Merani said. For the first time a smile broke out on her face, and she followed Mira to the garden wall. "May I touch one?"

"You can pick one if you like." Both of them sat on the edge of the fountain as Merani plucked a fellblossom and held it to her nose.

"I haven't seen one of these in the two years I've lived here," Merani said. "Such flowers don't grow so close to the sea. Where did you get them?"

"I had them brought from Fellheath a few years before the war," Mira said, brushing back her long dark hair. "I have flowers from all over the kingdoms, and if my flowerbeds were better weeded, I'd show them to you. But it's rather hot out here, don't you think? Would you like to come inside?"

Clutching the fellblossom, Merani nodded.

From the outside, Mira's house seemed little different from the other buildings of Ranath Drallm; it was built of white marble framed with wood and was crowned with a peaked thatch roof. But when Merani followed Mira through the door, she discovered that the ground floor room was several times ordinary size. It had a stone floor, a high roof, and polished walls hung with skycolored tapestries. At one end a stone stair swept upward toward a doorway crowned with the royal arms of Llarandil, a golden sun, draped beneath with silk. It seemed to Merani that this design was the motif for the entire room: it appeared in marble over the hearth, in mahogany on Mira's table and chairs, and in silver thread on a number of velvet pillows. The goblet, spoon, and bowl that Mira set in front of

Merani were silver and also stamped with the sun emblem; Merani was surprised that the peaches Mira brought were not marked, too.

"The sun is the symbol of the House of Llarandil, isn't it?" Merani asked while Mira poured cream over the peaches.

Mira nodded. "One of them. It's a lovely symbol. I have rather taken a fancy to it."

As she ate, Merani wondered how King Gion and the High Princess Geniolien would feel about a lesser house borrowing their insignia. But she said nothing. Instead she asked, "Is the Princess Geniolien back from Crywyll yet?"

Mira froze in mid-bite, then smiled. "She came back yesterday, I think. Have you seen her?"

"No, not except at a distance. And from what I could see of her, she didn't seem as beautiful as everyone says she is. In fact," Merani added, eyeing Mira, "you're much prettier than she is."

"Thank you." Mira dipped her spoon into her bowl. "But you shouldn't blame Geniolien for her reputation. It's been my experience that princesses are seldom seen as they actually are."

"She's heir to the throne as long as Gion is childless," Merani said. "I suppose that's why people get so excited about her."

Mira sighed. "King Gion would certainly make life much easier for Geniolien if he'd marry. As it is, every young man in the kingdoms is hoping she'll choose him as her escort tomorrow night at her homecoming feast."

"I wish," Merani said, "that one of those young men would stop thinking about the princess—"

"You haven't been asked yet?"

"No." Merani felt her lower lip protrude. "Have you?"

"Not exactly," Mira admitted, collecting the empty dishes. "But you and I both may be pleasantly surprised. Do you have a particular person in mind?"

Merani could not hide a smile.

"Let me guess. Is it that charming Captain Moleander I keep hearing so much about?"

"Me?" Merani burst out. "Me? Go with Captain Moleander? You can't have been here at Ranath Drallm long if you think that! Captain Moleander's taking Arien to the feast—or so she thinks. And if Arien couldn't go, he'd probably take Lady Mair, because she likes him and makes as many earthenware goblets for him as Arien makes tunics."

Mira's eyes lifted thoughtfully. "I see. I've heard of Lady Arien's needle. I do seamstress work myself, though I'll bet Arien does better. I've been working on a gown for a good seven months, but I can't decide how to finish it." Moving to an oak cabinet, Mira brought out a pale green gown that shimmered as if stars had been lodged in its weave.

Dropping a hand to touch her boyish leggings, Merani gasped, "It's beautiful!"

"Thank you. But I can't decide whether to use gold or silver thread for the trim. What do you think?"

"If I had a dress like that, I wouldn't think it needed either. Maybe," she went on, reflecting, "if I had a gown even half as nice, Ellari would ask me to the princess's feast."

"Ellari?" Mira repeated shrewdly. "Prince Ellari of Thrinedor? Is that who you want to ask you to the feast?"

Merani held her chin, hesitating, but then slowly nodded. "He's here from Thrinedor visiting his brother, Captain Berrian. When we all—Mole and Fflad and Arien and Berrian and I—went back to Thrinedor after the battle at Rathvidrian, Ellari took me riding and hawking. But since he's come to Drallm, he hasn't said more than hello to me." Merani narrowed her eyes. "I guess he's grown up, beyond paying attention to girls who don't wear beautiful dresses."

Mira folded the gown and replaced it in the cabinet. "You'd be quite lovely in a dress, too, Merani."

Looking at the arrow in her lap, Merani grimaced. "I like what warriors wear better," she said. "It's more practical."

"Practical for war, maybe," Mira returned. "But do you want to fight Ellari or do you want to go to the feast with him?"

Merani looked away from Mira and began tapping the arrow against the table. "If you want to know the truth," she said after a pause, "I don't have a gown. Not one. Arien's been promising to make me one for two years. But with the race she's had with Mair for Mole's attention, she hasn't had time. I suppose it's just as well. Even if I had a gown, no one would ask me to the feast."

"Gown and feast may both take care of themselves," Mira said. "Would you like some more peaches?"

"No, thanks," Merani said. Sighing, she got up. "And I better not stay any longer. I told Arien I'd be back from archery practice at noon to help with some sewing."

"You sew?"

"Only a little. I run errands mostly."

"In any case," Mira said, "I hope you can come back to-morrow. I could use some help sewing, too. And I have more peaches. Will you come?"

Standing near the door, Merani hesitated. "I guess so," she said, "if you want me to."

"I want you to," Mira said.

Once Merani left Mira's garden, her surroundings were much more familiar. She knew the layout of the fortress by heart. It was only the cluster of buildings behind her, toward the north gate, that she knew less well, for the royal apartments and council halls there were not places she could often venture into.

Merani soon came onto the grassy common, where she had been practicing archery, and she stopped long enough to pick up her bow. One of the High King's captains was drilling warriors in the direction of the Craftsmen's Quarter, crammed against the east wall. Westward lay, among other things, the Bards' Quarter, where Merani went only in the company of Fflad. In its libraries were as many of the works of the kingdoms as were known.

Neither of these places interested Merani as much as the long house against the south gate, the Hall of Captains. From the common she could see horsemen drawing in and out of the stable doors, and she thought she could hear her hawk, Cwyller, peeping in the mews. But she turned to the low-roofed wing of the house, near a great spruce tree, where she and Arien shared a room.

As Merani approached, she heard Arien's voice through the door. "But you'll have to admit that your father isn't being unreasonable, asking you to come back to Thrinedor. You've been here at Ranath Drallm for more than two years. You're Crown Prince of Thrinedor, remember?"

"I know." It was Berrian's voice. "But I don't want to go back—not yet. Not as quickly as Ellari says I have to go back. Can you believe that my father would send my little brother to tell *me* to come home?"

"If I were your father," Arien replied, "I would have sent Ellari sooner. After all, your father has been telling you to come home in letters for almost a year—Oh, hello, Merani."

Merani entered to find Arien and Berrian in seats on either side of the door. Arien was stitching at the hem of a garment that, compared with the memory of Mira's gown, seemed shoddy and dull.

"I was beginning to think you'd shot somebody with that bow of yours and been thrown in the castle dungeon. Where have you been?"

"Eating peaches," Merani said. "I'm sorry I'm late."

"You're not really late," Arien said. "I'm almost finished, anyway."

"Eating peaches?" Berrian asked. "Where?"

Merani threw her head back. "I shot an arrow into somebody's garden by mistake," she began, "but the whole thing ended up very pleasantly. I met a beautiful lady named Miralien."

"Miralien?" Arien said blankly. She leaned back in her chair, scratched her head, and looked at the patch of sky above the castle wall. "I know at least a dozen court ladies, but no Miralien—"

"Oh, she said she was new here. I don't know where she comes from. I'll have to ask her tomorrow."

"You'll have to show her to me at the feast," Arien said, a pin in her teeth. "That is," she added with a furious stitch, "if I finish this gown in time. Everyone will be wearing pale green, because it's the princess's favorite color. I don't want to look out of place."

Merani leaned against the doorpost, trying not to look at Arien's gown. "I couldn't help overhearing you," she told Berrian. "Will you be leaving?"

"Not if I can help it," Berrian said with a brooding frown. "But Ellari, the scoundrel, is determined to get me packing right after the feast."

"I don't see why you object to leaving," Merani said. "Gion made you a captain only temporarily, until you were needed at home. If I were you, I'd want to go home after two years."

"If you were Berrian," Arien corrected, "you'd be in love with Mair's sister, Gwenith, and you'd want to lock Ellari up to keep him from forcing you back to Thrinedor."

"All you have to do then," Merani returned, "is make Ellari want to stay here, too. He spends all day with the captains; get the High King to make him an honorary captain or something."

"That won't keep him," Berrian said. But he brightened. "Though I know what will. As my father always says, 'Hearts are chained more easily than bodies.' I'll introduce Ellari to one of the court ladies—better, I'll have him take one of them to the feast tomorrow night. Maybe then he won't be so anxious to leave."

Merani's eyes widened. She swallowed. "Yes. That's a good idea."

"I know," Arien put in. "Introduce him to Mair, since she won't be going otherwise."

Before Berrian could answer, Merani said, "What about you, Arien? Is Mole going to go with you?"

Arien laid the gown over the arm of a chair. "If he comes home from Eber Taranil on time. I wish he weren't gone so much: first to the marshes, next to Sharicom, now to Taranil. Sometimes I wish he'd never found that Sword in the mountain. It's caused nothing but trouble, and now it keeps him in the wilderness half the time!"

"High King Gion sends him," Berrian reminded her, "not the Sword."

"But if he didn't have the Sword, the High King wouldn't send him away so often." Arien plucked lint from her lap. "And now everybody I meet tells me Mole is likely to become High Captain when old Medwing gives up his post. *That* would be all we'd need—I'd never see Mole again! But at this point," she added with a wry grin, "I'd settle for his coming home before tomorrow night."

The night was dark and a storm was rising. Mole, lying awake in his blankets, felt the damp wind on his cheeks as he stared into the blackness above him. Leaves chattered in his ears, and twigs prattled against the tree trunks near his feet. From the distance came the sound of waves on the beach. Nearer, Wildfoal clicked restless hooves against the stones.

Mole pulled up his blankets and sighed to himself. "If only I'd left Eber Taranil before noon, I'd have been in Drallm by now."

"What you mean is you'd be trying to cross the River Thrine about now," said the voice of the Sword. "And with this storm, you'd be washed right into the sea."

"I may be washed into the sea as it is, if it rains."

Turning to his side, he tried to sleep. But the wind kept him awake in spite of his weariness; he listened to the storm for a long time before he dropped to sleep.

First he dreamed he was back in Taranil. He sat in the chamber of the lord of the city as the old man droned against a background of nightingale songs from the garden. Mole heard himself interrupt, "I can't sleep while you're talking. I can't sleep, I tell you! And if you don't let me leave soon, I'll drown trying to cross the river!" Abruptly the room darkened, the nightingales fell silent, and the lord of Taranil's body melted away into a dark wind. Only his face remained, the color of ice, and it grew until it spread across Mole's entire vision.

He woke with a start, but the pallid face remained. "Wildfoal," he said in sudden relief, pushing the horse's head aside. "Wildfoal, go away." As he turned over in his blankets, Wildfoal whickered behind him.

Sleep returned even more slowly than it had first come. Fingers knotted in his hair, he lay and listened to the thunder of the wind in the trees. Then, by and by, as the night deepened, the noises of the storm thinned away. It grew so quiet that Mole could hear the breath hissing in his throat and his heart drumming in his chest. He slept, yet it was not sleep; it was more a silence, a profound lull like a hollow in the wind or gap in the darkness. The stillness brought a dream, a dream unlike any other Mole had ever had, for it was as if he were fully awake gazing at a dark, age-dusted painting.

He saw a family sitting together in the firelight of a great stone hall. Three children, rich in dress, two boys and a girl, wore faces that reflected their mother, who sat in the orange glow of the hearth. Though her eyes looked downward, Mole saw that they were earth brown, the color of her hair and of a smooth clay goblet in her lap. Beside the woman stood a tall, dark man who wore a silver crown and held in one hand a staff that glowed faintly in the firelight. The man's eyes were so deep, so clear, so sorrowful that when Mole looked at them, the weave of the dream changed into something he could not remember afterward, except that it had to do with rain and wildflowers.

Rain began before first light, driving Mole from his dreams. Quickly he got up, shouldered his doeskin cloak, and fastened the Sword at his side. He saddled Wildfoal and rode from the clearing just as the first hints of dawn appeared.

"Beastly rain!" he growled as he urged Wildfoal into a canter on an open stretch of road. The drops blinded him. "And cold, too," he added. "I thought it was supposed to be summer. This feels like the beginning of snow!"

"When the weather's foul," the Sword replied, "there's a good chance that something else is foul, too."

In answer, Mole shook the rain from his face. He could scarcely see the sea beyond the headlands along the road, and then only in lines of white waves running toward the shore. The rain in his face kept him from seeing very far ahead, so he didn't push Wildfoal into a gallop.

When he saw a rider on the road late in the morning, he reined Wildfoal to a walk and squinted into the gloom. At first, seeing little more than a dark horse and a rain-gleaming cloak, he put his hand to the Sword. But at a dozen paces the horseman hailed him, and when Mole recognized the voice, he brought Wildfoal aflank of the other horse.

"Lord Morin!" Mole shouted.

"Captain Moleander! You're the last person I expected to meet on this road, though I knew you were coming back from Taranil. I spotted a goblin in the wood this side of the Thrine, so I almost expected you to be a sorcerer!"

Mole frowned. "The rain's left me in no mood for jests, my lord."

"Indeed," Lord Morin returned, steadying his horse, "I'm not amused myself, for I have to ride all the way to Candyll-beyond-Taranil. With this rain, I won't make it before dark. Terrible weather, isn't it?"

Mole nodded. "But why are you going to Candyll? I was there last week, and there didn't seem to be any trouble."

"I'm not going to Candyll to stop trouble." Morin's eyes flickered in the depths of his hood. "I'm going there to make trouble. Don't look at me like that, Mole. You'll understand when you get back to Ranath Drallm."

Mole felt Lord Morin's hand on his shoulder. "It isn't as serious as you fear," he said. "At least I don't think so. And at any rate, there's something bright in store for you at the end of the rain. I suggest you hurry on, if you want to be in time to receive it."

"Receive what?"

"I promised the High King I wouldn't tell you," Lord Morin said. Mole saw him suppress a smile. "And I always obey him."

Mole chuckled. "Well, then, you shouldn't have baited me

like that. Not that I want to make you disobey the High King, but does it have to do with the High Captain?"

"What High Captain? You know as well as I do that old Medwing has announced he wants to resign."

"That," Mole said, "is precisely what I mean. And you know it." Mole pushed the hair from hs eyes and went on, pensively, "You shouldn't encourage my ambition, Lord Morin. You know that I'm young and I've only been a captain two years."

"I also know," Morin returned, "that the High King is very fond of you. And Medwing was your age when High King Gion's father made him High Captain. Besides," he went on in a voice so low that Mole could barely hear it above the patter of the rain, "I don't know if I ever told you this, Mole, but you remind me very much of the man who was High Captain before Medwing, King Gion's uncle, Llaran." Lord Morin studied Mole through the rain. His eyes widened. "In fact—" He cut himself short. "No," he said, shaking his head, "no, I won't tell you that."

"You won't tell me anything," Mole countered. He straightened in his saddle. "And that's probably just as well. I don't like rumors."

Lord Morin's teeth flashed from his hood. "I never spread rumors."

Mole raised one hand in farewell and drew Wildfoal's head away from a clump of roadside grass.

"Wait!" Lord Morin said. "I almost forgot something. I have a message for you, Captain Moleander."

"Oh, indeed," Mole guessed. "From your daughter Mair?"

"She would have given me one if she'd known I would see you," Lord Morin answered.

"Who, then?"

"Your friend Fflad, the minstrel. He found me in the stables this morning, and he wasn't looking well, but he insisted that I give you this message if I saw you: he wants you to come to the Bards' Quarter to see him as soon as you get home. *As soon as*—he made that part very clear. He seemed quite excited."

"Bad news?" Mole said, watching the rain.

"I don't think so. He was smiling."

"With Fflad, that can be as bad." Mole steadied Wildfoal

and looked at Morin. "Thank you. And a good journey."

"Farewell, Moleander," Lord Morin shouted back. "And good luck."

The sounds of Lord Morin's horse were soon lost in the rain. Because the rain had slackened a little, Mole drove Wild-foal into a trot, then a gallop. The rain in his face made it sting, and he narrowed his eyes until water grew thick on his lashes.

"High Captain, indeed," he said.

"You're pleased, aren't you?" The Sword rattled against Mole's leg.

"But I don't know if I'll be chosen High Captain or not," Mole argued. Hoping the wind would drown out anything the Sword said, he strained forward in the saddle. "And to tell you the truth, I'm not so sure I'd want to be High Captain, even if I were chosen."

"Why not?"

Mole frowned. "Because I've seen Lord Medwing, that's why. He's less than twice my age, and he looks older than Gwarthan. But it's more than that, more than just the strain of being High Captain. No one likes to be around Medwing because he's so gloomy. All he talks about is war, about all his campaigns and battles and about all the men he's seen killed. I guess it weighs on you, all the men you've sent to their deaths, all the lives you've hacked away—"

"You've hacked away dozens of lives yourself, even without being High Captain," the Sword put in. "You killed goblins on Mon Ceth, outlaws in the Fell Downs, and that Pretender and his crowd of ruffians in the marshes."

"I don't regret killing goblins or sorcerers," Mole told the Sword, "and I had to fight the outlaws on Fellheath or be killed myself." He paused. The dripping trees alongside the road suddenly reminded him of the marsh in which he had led a campaign the summer before. "But," he said, "I sometimes see that Pretender in dreams. He wasn't very old, you know. He was younger than I am. And he was certainly mad. He really thought he was the High King, and when I went to him that morning in their camp..." Mole's voice trailed away into the rain. "... he seemed to think I was some kind of a...monster." Mole squeezed his eyes closed to force the vision of the Pretender from his mind.

"I don't see how being High Captain would make things any worse," the Sword persisted.

"It can't make them better."

"But you've always wanted to be High Captain. I know that."

Mole sighed. "Very much," he admitted. "But maybe I've grown wiser—or weaker. I dread it, Sword. I can see myself wearing Lord Medwing's face, looking through his eyes at the night, seeing fire in the stars and a skull in the moon..."

"Very vivid of you, my boy," the Sword said dryly. "But that's not the point. The point is that you will be offered the post of High Captain of the kingdoms, unless Lord Morin is simply taunting you. Don't you think Arien would rather marry Lord Moleander than a common captain?"

Mole considered. His answer whispered into the rain. "She would."

"There you have it, then," the Sword said, sounding pleased. It fell silent.

The road descended from the hills to a pleasant sweep along the beach toward the river mouth, and the clouds lifted to let Mole see the hill of Ranath Drallm. But he still scowled as he urged Wildfoal into the ford.

• 2 •

Binding and Loosing

"BLAST MOLE!" ARIEN declared. "If I'd known how often he'd be gone, I'd never have let him become a captain."

"I don't think he ever asked your permission," Merani returned. She sat by the quiet hearth and stared at Arien, standing in the door. "He loves being a captain."

"I know." Arien frowned. "It all started when he found that awful Sword. He fell in love with the dratted thing the moment he saw it, and he hasn't paid attention to anything else since. Oh, I knew he wouldn't be back from Taranil in time for the feast!"

"The feast isn't until dark," Merani said. "You have a few more hours—"

"Only a few," Arien muttered. "And even if he *does* get back in time, what will he look like, after riding all day in the rain?" She stalked to the fireplace, touched Merani's chair with her foot, then started back toward the door.

"It won't help to pace," Merani said.

"It can't hurt," Arien said. "And I'll go mad if I don't do something." She shot a glance at Merani. "Don't look so calm! If you'd spent weeks working on a gown and your escort was in Taranil, you'd be frantic, too."

Merani frowned down at her hands. "I guess," she said. Arien's gown, spread on a chair in the full light of the window, shimmered like a dawn-flecked sea. "It's a lovely dress, Arien. You embroider beautifully."

"For all the good it does me," Arien said, glaring at the gown. "I might just as well have saved myself a few pricked fingers."

"Mole will be back." Merani sighed. "He always makes it at the last moment. In fact, he might already be here. You ought to send someone to look for him."

"I already have. Ellari. And he ought to be back by now. Wait. I think I see him, coming across the lawn."

Chilled suddenly, Merani folded her arms. From the corner of her eye she saw a lanky shadow cross the threshold.

"Well," Arien asked, "did you find out anything?"

Ellari was panting. "Yes. I found out quite a bit. I found Mole. He's been in Drallm since noon."

"Since noon!" Arien thundered. "Did you see him?"

"Not exactly. Though I thought I did in the Bards' Quarter."

"And what were you doing in the Bards' Quarter?"

"Looking for Mole, of course. I found his horse in the stables and began asking the grooms where he'd gone. To the Bards' Quarter, they said, and then I kept getting lost in the passageways there."

"Then you didn't find Mole?"

"No." Ellari sounded uncomfortable. "But I wouldn't be worried if I were you. Mole will come here, and in plenty of time to take you to the feast."

Merani stood up. "Yes, he'll be here."

Ellari grinned when he saw her. "Merani, I didn't even notice you were here." Although Merani reddened, Ellari went on before she could greet him. "Now that I've done you a favor, Arien, maybe you can do me one. Tell me something. Be honest, now. Mair—the one Berrian says wants to go with me to the feast tonight—is she pretty?"

Arien gazed out toward the roofs of the feasting hall. "She could be called lovely, I suppose."

"Good." Ellari pushed a thumb under his belt. "The reason I'm asking—I know that's an odd question—is because, well, the plainest girls have a habit of falling in love with me. Not that plain girls are bad to have cook or sew for you, but when it comes to going to feasts, they ought to be pretty—"

Merani's hand went involuntarily to her cheek.

"If this girl's as beautiful as you say," Ellari went on, "she'll be the first beautiful girl ever to fall in love with me. Considering my past, I can't believe it could happen." Ellari paused, gathered his thoughts, and slammed a fist against the chamber wall. "Blast it, what I'm trying to say is that it's very strange I should meet up with such a girl after such a short time in Drallm. Especially since she noticed me before I noticed her."

"Yes, it is odd."

"Odd enough to make me suspicious of Berrian. If I didn't know better, I'd think he had set the whole thing up." A shadow crossed Ellari's face as he reconsidered. "Of course, Berrian is thoughtful, except when he argues about coming back to Thrinedor."

"Thrinedor," Arien said in a distant voice. "It was so lovely living in Thrinedor, when Mole wasn't always off on a campaign."

Ellari licked his lips. "The more I think about it, the more it doesn't really matter whether Berrian arranged this or not. I'll be feasting with a beautiful maiden just the same, won't I?"

"If you'll both excuse me," Merani said, brushing past Arien toward the door, "I have a visit to make before the feast."

Ellari's face lit. "Merani. Wait a moment."

She turned to him and offered a faltering smile.

"I've been meaning to ask you something since I got here," Ellari said. "But it kept slipping my mind."

"Ask anything you like."

"I'd like to do a little bow practice while I'm here at Drallm. Would you mind if I borrowed your bow? It has such good tension in the string."

"You're welcome to use it," Merani said, averting her eyes, "any time."

She hurried away across the common lawns, Ellari's face in her mind, until she reached the Royal Quarter. There the fragrances of blooming roses and newly cut grass made her think of Mira.

Her thoughts, however, scattered when a man came from behind a hedge and nearly knocked her down. Instead of apologizing, the man shook a finger at her and bellowed, "Out of my way! I've had enough of fickle women!"

"Don't shout at me," Merani retorted, feeling her cheeks flush, "or you might find out just how fickle a woman can be!"

To this the man glowered, then stormed away behind another hedge.

"How do you like that," Merani growled, bustling on.

The first thing she noticed as she peered through the gate into Mira's garden was that someone had plucked some of the tulips and thrown them into the fountain. The rest of the yard was as she remembered it, sleepy and fragrant.

Mira soon appeared in her chamber doorway. Seeing Merani, she hurried to the gate and let her in.

"Did I come at a bad time?" Merani asked. She noted that Mira was breathing hard and that her forehead was damp.

"No, no. Come in, Merani. I'm glad you came."

"You look hot—" Merani fumbled for words. "That man, was he here?"

"Man?" Mira said blankly, hurrying Merani past the flowers in the pool. "I'm afraid I don't know who you mean. And besides, it doesn't really matter, does it? Now, I have something to show you."

Merani followed Mira up a broad stone staircase into a long upper chamber. The glare of the sun through the windows thus blinded Merani, so that she could see little more than the size of the room. But gradually, as Mira took her toward the windows, the sun dipped behind the trees, and she could see her surroundings. Richly decorated, like the lower room, the upper chamber displayed a dozen sky-colored tapestries embroidered with the royal sun of Llarandil. A bed stood near the windows with the same emblem carved on an oak headboard and on the woodwork of a loom, a table, and shelves that held worn-looking books. But Merani saw none of this for long, for in the center of the room was a high-backed chair across which was draped the most beautiful gown Merani had ever seen. The gems sewn along its hems glittered like stardust.

Mira halted and straightened. She smiled as Merani's eyes widened. "Now, Merani," she said, "you don't have an excuse to miss the feast."

Merani blinked at her. "It . . . it's for me?"

"Look at the size of it," Mira replied. "It wouldn't fit me."

"It wouldn't fit me, either," Merani said. "No gown fits someone more used to tunics and arrows. I'd be afraid to wear it."

"You'd be surprised," Mira said, "to find out how much the woman changes to fit the clothing she wears. Do you want to try it on?"

In no time at all, Merani stood in front of a polished mirror, smoothing the gown. Her appearance, she had to admit, stunned her.

"Do you like it?" Mira asked, touching her shoulder.

Merani nodded to her image in the looking glass. But suddenly the image frowned. "Mira, I can't take this gown. I appreciate your offering it, but I won't be able to use it. I'm not even invited to the feast. I don't have anyone to go with!"

"Go by yourself, then."

"By myself?" Merani laughed. "The only person allowed to go by herself is the High Princess Geniolien."

"I'm going by myself," Mira stated. "If you'd like, we can go by ourselves together, if you know what I mean."

"But they won't let us!"

"Oh, but they will," Mira said. Keeping her eyes on Merani's reflection, Mira pushed back her hair to reveal the full oval of her face. "Or at least they'd better let us," she added. "After all, they keep calling it *my* feast."

Mole opened the door and peered into the room.

At first he thought it was dark and vacant, but a spark of daylight caught his eyes, and he realized that the room was lit by a single narrow window facing a shadowed wall and by a small candle burning on a table by the door. The effect was not darkness but dimness, a dimness thick like dust and clouded like fog. The inside of the room smelled dry and musty, something like a long-empty stable warmed by the sun.

"Fflad?" Mole probed. "Fflad? Are you there?"

He was surprised to hear an answer. Feebly, "Mole?"

Clutching his riding cap, Mole moved over the threshold. "I wasn't sure this was your room, Fflad. It's so dark. You always have a bright fire going and friends coming in and out. What's wrong?"

"This room's always dark in the afternoon," Fflad's voice answered. "And it's too hot to build a fire. How was Taranil?"

Mole forced himself to chuckle. "How can Taranil be?"

A pause. "Well, I'm glad to see you back. Sit down, Mole."

By this time Mole could see a chair beside Fflad's bed and beyond, a few familiar objects: Fflad's lyre, Fflad's shelf of lore books, and Fflad's traveling cloak, thick with dust, on a peg near the window. When he grew accustomed to the unsteady light of the candle, he saw that Fflad lay on the bed, one knee cocked up, arms hugged across his stomach. His face, unless it was the light, was as colorless as clay, though his eyes reflected steadily the movements of the candle flame.

"You're ill," Mole said.

Fflad smiled slightly; the beginning of a laugh escaped his lips. "You're quite right. But it's my own fault. I worked myself into it. I knew I was going to get sick from all the excitement, but I just couldn't make myself slow down. Still, looking at it on the bright side, I won't have to go to that feast and ruin my fingers by strumming all night—"

"What excitement?"

"I don't know if I dare tell you about it," Fflad said. He lifted a hand toward Mole. "If I do, I may keep you here so long Arien will never forgive me."

"Arien will wait. Tell me."

Fflad smiled; a nuance of color returned to his face as he lifted his head, reached under his pillow, and took out something he held up to the light of the window. "Remember this, Mole?"

"Of course," Mole said. "That's the hoop you found in the outlaws' saddlebag on Fellheath."

"Yes. And I always thought it was magical. I *knew* it was. I've carried it around since we found it, thought about it, dreamed about it, even when a dozen experiments seemed to say the hoop was nothing more than a piece of wire. But while you were gone to Taranil, I discovered its power."

"What does it do? Make you sick?"

"No!" Fflad's voice edged on hoarseness. "I'll show you. Mole, hold the other side of it, will you?"

Mole groped, caught the rim of the ring, and squeezed it into his palm, half expecting it to send fire through his veins.

"Nothing's happening," he said in a moment.

"That's a pity," Fflad said quietly. "I've always thought of you as my brother."

"I don't understand."

"Neither did I, at first. I found the power of the hoop unexpectedly. I had been looking at it one afternoon and had left it on my table. That evening, Captain Celain and Captain Paladain paid me a visit, to ask me about an old ballad or something. One of them noticed it, and both of them picked it up at the same time. The ring began to glow as if it had been heated up in a smith's forge. It didn't burn them, but it seemed to flame as long as both of them held it. And when one or the other let go, or when I touched it, it immediately stopped glowing and looked just as you see it now."

Mole took the hoop from Fflad. "This is a binding ring, then," he said in wonder, "because Celain and Paladain are brothers. I've heard of such things before, but I thought they were only legends. And, well, I thought they were more spectacular-looking."

"It's not just *a* binding ring," Fflad said, propping himself up on his elbows, "it's *the* binding ring, the Binding Ring of Merwnedd, who was one of the Seven Wizards of Fellheath. I know because the moment I saw what happened, I looked through every lore book in Ranath Drallm. There's only one binding ring mentioned in all the chronicles of the kingdoms, and this hoop fits the description perfectly."

"Then why didn't Gwarthan realize what it was when you showed it to him? He learned his art from the Fellheath wizards, didn't he?"

"Maybe he was too flustered to recognize it," Fflad suggested, "or maybe he'd never seen it before. It doesn't matter. Anyway, I've sent a message to him about it. He's in southern Crywyll, on some dark errand for the High King—"

"Do you realize the power something like this has?" Mole interrupted.

The sideboards of the bed creaked as Fflad pushed himself to a sitting position. "Yes, of course. Do you think I hid it in my oak chest as soon as I found out what it was? No, I went everywhere with it. I found that it has a different intensity of glow for almost all relationships; it seems to work on a principle of common blood. It can tell sisters as well as brothers. It can bind grandfather and grandson, nephew and uncle, great-grandmother and great-granddaughter. And if family relationships are more distant, it still glows slightly. But I never told any of the people what the ring was, at least not more than I had to. I didn't want anybody to take the ring away from me. Not until I had used it to find out the thing I've always wanted to know most."

An old longing whispered in Mole's mind. "Your parentage," he said.

"Mine and yours and Arien's."

Mole gripped the arm of the chair, battling sudden dizziness.

"Are any of our parents here," he breathed, "here in Drallm?"

"No," Fflad replied, "at least not any of mine among those I've tested. But that's why I wanted you to come." Fflad's eyelids drifted down momentarily. "I have found my parents."

For a long time Mole could not speak. "Fflad," he whispered at length. "Fflad, are you sure?"

Fflad nodded slightly. "Beyond all reasonable doubt."

"But how, if they're not here at Drallm? How?"

Leaning back against the headboard, Fflad sighed. "How, indeed," he said. "Sometimes I wonder myself. Again, it was quite an accident. Mole, I never dreamed—not all the time we lived in the cave on Mon Ceth or at the academy at Ranath Thrine—I never thought that Arien and I—"

"You and Arien?" Mole stammered. "You're brother and sister?"

"Not just brother and sister, Mole. Twins."

Mole gaped. He wanted to believe, yet he couldn't. "How can it be?" he said. "How can it be, Fflad? Rhawn found you and Arien at different times, in different places. How can it be?"

Gaunt with earnestness, Fflad's face mirrored Arien's. "It is. I know it is. Look at me and think of Arien. Think of how our voices sound. We're surely about the same age, and when Arien touched the ring, it shone more brightly than it ever had before. And there's more. Because Arien and I are twins, I was able to find our parents. *Our* parents. Listen to the sound of that, Mole."

"Your parents," Mole croaked. He tried to smile. "Go on."

"I simply had to look in the kingdom chronicles to find someone who bore and lost twins about seventeen years ago. I searched the libraries for two days without sleep. I found nothing at first. But I wouldn't let myself give up, and finally I stumbled on an old collection of histories written by the Lord of Eber Seador."

"Seador? Your parents came from Thrinedor?"

"No. Not from Thrinedor. Maybe I'd better explain the story as I understand it. It seems there was an Aelenwaith lord named Escandrin who married a coast princess named Ingra, in the days when Ammar made winter in Pesten. When Ingra had twins, a boy and a girl, Lord Escandrin decided to take them to a cousin of his, Llandrin, Lord of Seador, for some kind of ceremony. He got to Drallm by ship from Aelenwaith, but because he was too impatient to wait for another ship, he took a guard of warriors and traveled the land route to Seador through the Thrine Valley. A treacherous member of the company deserted them near Mon Ceth, taking with him Lord Escandrin's daughter. Escandrin tried to track him but couldn't because goblin war bands hounded him across the border into Thrinedor. Escandrin spent six months in Eber Seador, but instead of returning by ship to Aelenwaith as he had planned, he returned through the Vale of Thrine to search for his daughter. But he and all of his company, including his infant son, were never heard from again and were supposed to have all been killed."

"Six months," Mole mused. "Fflad, Rhawn found you six months after he found Arien."

Keeping his eyes on Mole, Fflad nodded. "My father, Escandrin, is dead. But my mother, Ingra; she should still be living in Aelenwaith—"

Mole leaped to his feet and caught Fflad, wordless, in a sudden fierce embrace. He dragged Fflad to his feet, then released him to squeeze his shoulders and laugh into his eyes. "Fflad! Your parents. And your mother perhaps still alive!"

"It's a lovely thought," Fflad said, "even if one is very tired. I can hardly believe it, Mole, even now—" Fflad cut himself short when he saw shadows as well as joy on Mole's face. "And Mole, we'll use the ring to find your parents, too."

Mole touched his hand to his chin. "I think I saw them," he muttered, "in a dream last night—unless the man was I."

"What was that, Mole?"

Mole shook back his hair and grinned. "I said that I'm awfully glad for you. And happy for Arien. How did she take the news?"

Fflad's eyes fell. "She doesn't know."

"You haven't told her?"

"No. And you must promise not to tell her."

"Fflad, why not?"

"It's been hard to keep the secret," Fflad said, "but I thought it would be wiser not to, in case . . . in case . . ."

"In case you're wrong? But how could you be?"

"Easily. It's easy to prove what you want to believe, Mole. And I've never wanted to believe anything more. I could have overlooked an important passage or imagined a helpful detail. And even if I'm right, what if Lady Ingra of Aelenwaith is gone or dead? Can I promise Arien a mother and bring her a wraith?"

"I see what you mean," said Mole. "And I agree. But you must send for Ingra as quickly as possible and use the binding ring to see if she's your mother."

"Yes," Fflad answered. "And quickly. But you can't send messages to Aelenwaith. I've tried. That's why I wanted to see you. Mole, we've been friends for a long time, and I've asked you to do dozens of favors. But none as big as what I ask you to do now."

Mole folded his arms. "I've never refused you a favor."

"I know. But you can refuse this one if you like. I'll understand. There's a rumor that you are to replace Medwing as High Captain. And with a new war brooding in the west—"

"Ask your favor," Mole interrupted. "Please."

"I'd go to Aelenwaith myself, but I'm in no health for a voyage." Mole noticed how prominent the candle glow made Fflad's cheekbones look. "The healing masters say I have a sickness that may take weeks to heal—my sleepless nights in the library did nothing to improve it—so I won't be able to travel until the beginning of autumn, when the squalls begin. If we have the early autumn the weather masters are predicting, I may not be able to leave for Aelenwaith until next spring. By that time—"

Mole broke in, "I understand. You want me to go to Aelenwaith. You want me to find Lady Ingra and bring her back to Drallm with me."

Fflad nodded. "As soon as you can."

Mole walked to the window and stared out into the collecting shadows. "A week's voyage to Aelenwaith, a week on the island, and a week to come back," he murmured. "That's not much longer than I was gone to Taranil, and it's for a better cause." Suddenly Mole seemed to see in the reflections on the window glass the image of the ash staff, which he now remembered he had left as a paperweight in his room. "Rhawn told me once," Mole went on, "that the only way to find yourself is to look for somebody else."

"You'll go to Aelenwaith for me then?"

"I'll ask the High King's leave tonight," Mole said, "on one condition."

Fflad blinked at Mole.

Mole laughed. "On the condition that you'll excuse me to

leave you now. I've got to find Arien. She'll be frantic or she'll have found somebody else to take her to the High Princess's feast."

The light in the corridor stung Mole's eyes when he closed Fflad's door. The sapphires of the Sword's scabbard sparkled with the same brilliant color. "Now that you mention Arien," said the Sword, "don't you think that when she finds out she's from a noble Aelenwaith family, she'll feel odd about going to feasts with a common orphan?"

Mole didn't answer, but he went down the first flight of steps in hardly more than a bound and nearly flew through the window beyond the landing. All he could think of, as he clattered down the long staircases, was that everyone, including the king, called High Captain Medwing a lord.

Never in her life, Merani thought, had she seen anything so beautiful. She had often seen lovely things, like Cwyller's snowflake wings against a bright summer sky, frost on blooming heather, and tufts of cloud collecting between the toes of the mountains. Yet even her most vivid memories of Fellheath seemed dull in comparison to the spectacle now arrayed before her in the High King's feasting hall.

The hall itself was so long and high that Merani imagined herself outdoors instead of in; the great vault, she thought, was something like a clearing in the forest. The buttresses and arches were the color and shape of birch trunks with branches arching to meet overhead. The hundreds of candles burning from iron rings near the ceiling seemed to be stars, and their smoke and the smoke from the other fires of the hall gathered in the peak of the roof to form a cloud, through which the moon glittered, riding in a high window. The brightly dressed people seating themselves at the tables became fanciful folk, even though Merani knew most of them, for being seated beside the High Princess on the dais made Merani imagine herself to be a kind of benign magical queen.

The jewels on the sleeve of her gown glittered as she tapped Princess Geniolien on the shoulder. "You were right," she said, "it is beautiful. Your brother must be glad to have you back, the way he's decorated the hall."

"Speaking of my brother," Geniolien replied, "I wonder where he is? It's not like him to be late, and the hall's almost full."

Indeed, few seats remained, and the serving girls had already begun to pour ale. Near the back of the hall, the Chief Minstrel paced among his harpists, who began sounding tentative runs. Merani saw a pair of her fellow archers near the doors; she hoped somehow they would see her, though she realized they might not recognize her.

A moment later she saw Berrian and Gwenith, hand in hand, working their way along the wall toward empty seats to her right. Her eyes flicked away, then returned, for behind them came Ellari. Merani bit her finger when she recognized Mair at his side. Mair, wearing an attractive earth-colored gown, was almost as lovely as Princess Geniolien. Mair's clay-brown eyes searched the hall, probably looking for Mole, but returned to Ellari, who smiled at her before edging back into the crowd.

Merani narrowed her eyes and began bunching the edge of the tablecloth in her fingers. She stared when she felt a hand on her arm.

"Merani," said Geniolien, "Merani. I don't see Captain Moleander here. Are you sure he was planning to come?"

"I'm sure he was," Merani returned blankly, "but I don't see him either. Maybe he'll come in late. He came back from Taranil just this afternoon, you know."

Geniolien smiled uneasily. "I do hope he comes, Merani. Because there's a rumor he's to be chosen High Captain," she added hurriedly when she read Merani's gaze. "I mean, if he's to be made a noble, he really ought to be here—"

"Pardon me," Merani said, "but someone on that nearest table is trying to get your attention."

"I know," Geniolien said between her teeth, pretending to look away. "He's been staring at me since he came in."

"That's the same man who almost knocked me down on the way to your garden today!" Merani exclaimed. "It's the one who shouted at me."

"Beast!" Geniolien hissed. She bent to adjust the hem on her gown. "Merani, that's Prince Redwar of Crywyll, the man who courted me all the time I studied in his father's kingdom. He has a temper the color of his hair and an ambition to match."

Merani glanced between Geniolien and the prince. "He *followed* you back from Crywyll?" Merani whispered. "By Fifran, Geniolien, you're the High Princess. If you don't want him here, have your brother send him home!"

"I can't have him sent away," Geniolien said back. "He's

here for a secret war council my brother's having in the morning. At least that's why he says he's here."

"He seems to be the kind of man my father would have set the dogs on at home," Merani said. "Is he in love with you?"

"No. No, he's not in love with me. He's in love with my crown." Sparks from the nearest torch sparkled in Geniolien's eyes when she looked up. "And it took me almost two years to realize that."

Merani watched Geniolien and Redwar exchange cold stares until a sudden silence brought her attention to the door behind the dais. As the talking dwindled away, the assembly rose to their feet and turned their faces toward the dais door.

To a silence made brittle by the crackle of flames, the High King entered. Merani thought he was taller than she remembered him, but it may have been his posture, swift and erect, his even strides, his hard-held chin. He was dressed, as was his custom, in a simple blue shift belted with black leather. He wore a short cape of the same color. Only a simple medallion stamped with Llarandil's sun gave token of his rank.

"Friends," the High King said, "welcome." His voice boomed against the most distant pillars of the hall and quieted the snap of the flames. Yet it was really no louder than a whisper. "Friends. It is my honor to host you at this feast to welcome my sister Geniolien, who has just returned from Crywyll. We are grateful to have her back with us."

Someone began clapping in the back of the hall, and the crowd joined in. Geniolien smiled and whispered something to the High King when the applause did not end immediately. Merani saw Prince Redwar's gloves beating a slower rhythm, stone eyes fixed on Geniolien. And she thought she saw Mole and Arien come through the door as the clapping ended.

"We all know the purpose for this feast," the High King said, "so I won't ruin Geniolien's homecoming with a long speech." An attempt at applause, from the minstrels and the archers near the doors, scattered into silence. "We will have dancing and feasting once I have made a few announcements." The High King paused, as if to make certain all were listening. "First, there will be a council for all captains and lords in my rooms tomorrow morning after breakfast."

The silence deepened. Looking at the High King's face, Merani saw it darken. "The council can wait for sunlight," the High King continued, "and at present, I have a more pleasant announcement. Is Lord Medwing here?"

Several of the lords at the first table looked at one another. "High Captain Medwing excuses himself, Your Majesty," one of them said. He added, eyes downward, "At least I'm sure he would if he could, sire."

"What? Has Lord Medwing left Drallm, my lords?"

Two of the lords nodded, and one shook his head. Suddenly the gloom on the lords' faces spread to the High King's, and he said heavily, in a voice only Merani and Geniolien could hear, "Some nights have no stars, Medwing. If only—" He cut himself short and sighed. "Now. Are the minstrels ready?"

"Gion," Geniolien broke in, "you have one other announcement to make."

"Oh, yes," said the High King with a shallow laugh. "I do have one more thing to say. I've chosen a new man to replace Lord Medwing now that he's retired. I think most of you know already whom I have chosen. But the new High Captain has already proved his loyalty to me and his ability to fight my battles. He is young, but so am I, and I dare say he's a better swordsman than I am. Captain Moleander. Are you here?"

Merani saw Mole stand up. He raised his hand to the High King, who smiled and motioned for him to approach the dais. Mole was quite red as he walked forward, and he bowed clumsily in front of the king.

Geniolien looked at Mole. "Might we start the dancing now?" she asked Gion. "I haven't danced for such a long time." She smiled at Mole.

"Let the first march begin, then," the High King said, and he sat down and began talking to Mole. The Chief Minstrel struck up a chord on his lyre, and the other musicians joined him with flutes and harps in an old melody.

Stepping from the dais, High Princess Geniolien touched Mole's shoulder. "I beg your pardon, Captain Moleander, but it is traditional for the High Princess to choose her escort for the first march. And I would be honored if you would dance with me."

Mole looked at the High King, then at Geniolien, then at Merani. "But I hardly know how to dance, Your Majesty."

"You can't say that, Moleander. I've seen you at sword-play."

Paling, Mole looked at the crowd, who had cleared an opening among the tables and were watching with interest. "Very well," he said, a little gruffly. "It would be a pleasure."

He held his hands toward her, and she slipped a hand across his shoulder and coupled her free hand with his. The two began their march somewhat awkwardly, for Mole looked at nothing but his feet, and Geniolien looked at nothing but Mole. Merani watched them until other couples joined them in the space between the tables.

Feeling a tap on her shoulder, Merani turned around. Prince Redwar stood beside her, eyebrows drawn. He watched the dancers even when he spoke to Merani. "Would you like to dance?"

Merani smiled sweetly. "Of course, Your Majesty. But not with you. Thank you for asking."

"Dance with me, I say."

Merani folded her arms and smirked. "I'm sorry, Prince Redwar, but I'm a fickle woman. Remember?" As he started away, frowning, she spied Ellari leading Mair into the dance, and she almost wished in spite of her dislike for the Crywyll prince that she had danced with him.

The Chief Minstrel soon ended the song with a prolonged chord.

"I propose that the next march be in honor of the new High Captain," someone shouted as the couples moved away to the tables.

"Hear, hear!" roared some of the young captains.

A new piece of music began, but Mole, standing alone on the floor, did not move until the High King nodded at him. Then he went to the back of the hall, took Arien from the crowd, and began to dance with her. Princess Geniolien hurried up the steps to the dais; she whispered something to the High King, then left the hall.

And it was only a few minutes later, when Merani turned around to watch the dance again, that she realized Mole and Arien had left as well, for they were not among the dancers.

It was dark beneath the beech trees except for light from the windows of the feasting hall and the bright cracks in its doors. Away from the music and laughter, the fortress seemed withdrawn and silent. A single window glittered among the stars in the Bards' Quarter; a lone dog howled in the common.

"I'm sorry to drag you away like that," Mole said, stopping at a bend in the walk, "but I had to get away. I've never danced with a princess before. Especially not a High Princess."

"You've never danced before at all," Arien said. "If you want to know, you looked quite silly."

"I did feel silly at first," Mole admitted. "But during the dance, I almost forgot I was in front of all those people. Oh, come on, Arien. Don't frown like that. It's not like you to be jealous. It's not as if I were going to *marry* the High Princess. I simply danced with her. And she chose me only because I'd just been made High Captain—"

"You're blind if you think that," Arien said. "She was waiting for you to dance with her again, you know."

"I didn't notice. I was too busy looking for you."

Arien bowed her head. "I know. I'm sorry, Mole. It's just that you've been away so long. I hardly see you anymore. I was afraid...I was afraid something had happened—"

"Nothing's happened, Arien. Almost nothing."

"You mean what happened inside. Now you're High Captain."

Mole closed his eyes and pushed his hands together. "I'm not going to be High Captain."

She blinked at him, not daring to react. "Mole," she said, slowly, "are you sure? I know you want to be."

"That doesn't matter," he said. He turned away. "And if I did everything I wanted to, I'd be dead by now. My bones would be bleaching in some pitfall on Misty Mountain. I used to think my life was charmed, but I realize now that it isn't, no more charmed than Lord Medwing's was—"

"*Was?*" Arien said. "Mole—"

"He's dead," Mole said, shivering a little. "He's dead. They didn't want to announce it at the feast, but he is. I haven't heard how he died, but I think he killed himself."

"Killed himself? Mole, how do you know?"

"I'm not as blind as you say," Mole said, frowning toward the feasting hall. "I read it all in the faces of those lords. And I might have guessed it without them. The High Captain isn't an office. It's a madness."

"Mole," Arien said. She linked her hands around his arm. "You shouldn't confuse the office and the person. For all we know, Medwing may have gone mad whether he was the High Captain or not."

"No, Arien. It wasn't Medwing's madness, and even if it was, it has begun to work on me already. I admired Medwing once. I wanted to be like him. But I began to see his unhappiness. And now I know I can't buy nobility by selling my sanity. I won't barter my happiness for greatness. I won't be responsible for ten thousand deaths, of friends as well as enemies. I won't be High Captain."

"You don't have to be," Arien said. "Mole, I'm the last person to encourage you to use that Sword of yours any more than you have to. I don't want you to be High Captain if it will drive you mad. But I think you're a bit blinded, maybe, by the shock of Medwing's death. Being named High Captain is a great honor. You ought to think it over. The thing I don't understand, Mole, is that since you're a captain already, why will being High Captain make it any worse?"

"The Sword asked me the same thing," Mole said.

Arien pressed her lips. "Then maybe the Sword is right for once. I mean, I don't want you to be away from Drallm more than you already are, but I do want you to be happy. I've known you for a long time, and I know that down deep you won't be happy *unless* you are High Captain. You won't kill any more people as High Captain than you do as a captain."

"Then I'd better stop being a captain," Mole said.

"Somebody has to kill goblins," Arien said. "Somebody has to fight the wars that keep these kingdoms safe from outlaws and hawk kings and sorcerers. Someone has to be a swordsman, Mole, and so long as you are one, why not reap the rewards?"

Mole smiled bitterly. "You saw Medwing's reward."

"But all your life you've wanted to be something like a High Captain," Arien reminded him. "Don't throw away your dreams just because you're upset. What would you do if you weren't a captain?"

"Go to Aelenwaith," Mole said.

"Aelenwaith?" Arien stormed. "What's in Aelenwaith?"

Mole turned around and looked at her. "I've been meaning to tell you all evening," he said, "that I'm planning to go to Aelenwaith soon, as soon as I can arrange for a ship to take me."

"An errand for the High King?"

"No. But I think he'll let me go. I'm going to ask him tonight to let me quit the captaincy—at least for a while."

"But why go to Aelenwaith?"

"I can't tell you," Mole said. "I promised."

"Who did you promise?" Arien demanded.

"I can't tell you that, either." Mole held a finger to her lips. "And, no, you can't come with me, so don't bother to ask. Let me explain. I'm going because I need to think. I need to get away. I'm going because of someone I love; I'm going for you. And I'm going for the staff, not the Sword."

Arien nodded slowly, then walked away from him. "I won't try to discourage you, Mole. I'll trust you. Though trusting you may be a frightening thing at best."

Moving to her, Mole turned her face toward him. "I won't be long in Aelenwaith. I can promise you that much. And when I get back, if I've come to grips with the ghost of Medwing, if I've learned something—" He faltered for lack of words. "If things are the same between us, maybe we can—"

"What do you mean by *if* things are the same between us?" Arien said tartly. "Why wouldn't they be?"

"Things happen," Mole said evasively. "Things happen to change people."

"I don't know what you're talking about," Arien said, narrowing her eyes. "But I do know that look in your eye. You've been looking at me like that all evening, as if I were somebody you'd never seen before. In fact, you're beginning to act as strange as Fflad has lately. Have you been talking to Fflad?"

Mole turned his head away, then nodded.

"Are you going to Aelenwaith," Arien probed, "because of something Fflad said?"

Again Mole nodded.

"I knew it!" Arien slapped her hands together. "And it has to do with that hoop-thing Fflad found in Fellheath, doesn't it? Has that hoop discovered some treasure in Aelenwaith?"

Mole smiled. "You might say that." He laughed. "But it is a secret, at least until I bring it back to Drallm."

"Is Fflad going with you?" Arien asked.

"He would, but he isn't well. Haven't you seen him lately? He looks as brittle as a birch branch; the healing masters say he's got something that may take weeks to recover from. And this excitement about Aelenwaith hasn't helped him much. You'll have to take care of him while I'm gone."

"Of course I will," Arien said. "Why wouldn't I?"

"Just remember that Fflad's the only family you'll have while I'm gone," Mole admonished. "Treat him as if he were your brother."

"He is, isn't he?"

Mole blinked. "Arien," he began, "you—"

"What I mean," Arien interrupted, "is that I've always thought of you as brothers, all of you I grew up with on Mon Ceth. Just as I'll always think of Rhawn as a father—"

Mole made no answer. Watching the moon glide among the branches of the trees above, he remembered how moonlight had looked on the snowdrifts of Mon Ceth. "Arien," he said after a while, "do you want to go back to the feast?"

She shook her head and took his arm. "I'd rather go for a walk, I think. I'm not really hungry, and after all," she explained, "I may not get another chance to be with you for a long time. In fact," she said, squinting through the leaves, "I may never get another chance to be with you like this."

"Now look who's coming up with strange ideas," Mole chuckled. But he felt suddenly cold. "Come on. Shall we go to the river?"

They walked across the empty lawns, between empty buildings, out a shadowed gate onto the castle hill. Stars burned and wheeled above them; they seemed so near that Mole felt he and Arien were walking among them, reaching out for them, feeling the warm wind of their fires in their faces. All earth was black, and all sea and sky bright with lights. A wind humming across the river brought smells of willows and grass and mountain flowers.

They followed the river to the sea, and the sea to the stone harbor, where shadow ships rocked under the glare of the moon. Then as the night coursed toward midnight, they turned their backs to both sea and stars and climbed the castle hill again to the gate.

"We'll never see such stars as these again," Mole said.

Arien held his shoulder and touched her cheek to it. "No, never such stars. Dawn is coming."

Mole looked down at her in wonder because he knew that dawn was still far off. But he said good-bye and started back toward his own room. He had gone halfway across the common before he looked back to glimpse a rectangle of light beyond the trees. Arien was standing in it, watching him go.

All at once Mole wondered whether he should go to Aelenwaith or not. But when Arien's door closed, he saw Fflad's face again as he had seen it through the binding ring.

He went to his own room, passed through the door soundlessly, snatched the Sword from his bed, and strapped it around his waist. He paused long enough to see Berrian's head and shoulders above his blankets in the moonlight from the window, then he crept out again into the night, bound for the Royal Quarters.

Faint lights danced on the windows of the feasting hall, and peering in, he saw only a few servants collecting crockery from the tables. So he hurried on, past the darkened hall of thrones, taking a twisted path between hedges that led into the very heart of the fortress.

In the blackness, the passages of the inner palace seemed a maze, and Mole began to feel as if he were in a dream. He found himself stumbling up steps he usually took in quick strides, groping in galleries where he had often run. But at last he came to a familiar chamber, where a lamp burned within.

He knocked.

"Come in," said a voice. Mole lifted the latch and entered.

High King Gion sat behind a low table in a circle of yellow lamplight. His medallion had been set aside; it sparkled dully near his hand. When the door closed, he set down his quill and looked up. The creases around his eyes softened when he saw it was Mole.

Mole bowed. "I'm sorry to come to you so late, sire," he said, "but it's important."

"You don't need to apologize, Lord Moleander." The king leaned back in his chair, stroking the hair at his temples. "And after all these years, you don't have to call me 'sire.' Gion will do. After all, you are my High Captain now."

Mole looked at the floor. "That's what I've come to talk about."

"Ah," the High King said, "you've heard about Medwing. Sadness blights the happiest occasion. Not that I thought the old lord could last much longer, what with his old wounds opening again and his bad dreams. But he died in his sleep, in the care of the healing masters."

"Then he didn't take his own life?"

"Is that what concerned you?" Gion nodded to himself. "He didn't wield the knife that killed him, if that's what you mean. But he didn't want to live, either."

"Then," Mole said icily, "it is the same thing."

Gion looked at him for a long time. "You don't wish to be High Captain. I can see that."

"Maybe I'm wrong," Mole replied. "Maybe I need time to

think. But no, I don't want to be High Captain. In fact, I have a further wish. I want to leave the captaincy."

The High King's lips tightened, greying. "For good, Moleander?"

"I don't know. I hope not, sire—Gion—but I can't tell." Mole sighed. "I'm very confused. You can see that. I need to get away. If you can arrange a ship for me, I'd like to leave for the Isle of Aelenwaith as soon as possible."

"I can have a ship ready for you tomorrow."

"Thank you."

The High King leaned forward on the table. His face in the full light of the lamp seemed age-worn. "Moleander, tell me; are you leaving because of something I've done? Have I treated you unfairly? Is there anything I can do to change your mind?"

Mole grinned wryly. "The answer is three times no. Sire, you haven't done anything but good for me these two years. I'm grateful for that. And I'll come back—maybe to the captaincy."

"I won't bar your way, then. But I'll miss you both as High Captain and as a swordsman."

"You have enough men to do both," Mole said.

"Enough in numbers," Gion said. Then he fell silent.

When the wick of the lamp had grown dimmer, the High King spoke again. "War is coming. If the council tomorrow decides to act, I will muster the coastlands in a week and begin a march into the west."

"War?" Mole fought for words. "In the west? I've heard rumors, but I never guessed . . . Sire, if you command me, I will—"

"I don't like to command. Though I may need your help before the end, I won't keep you back. For I think it will be a short war. The danger in the west is only beginning; it is not at its apex of power as was the peril in Vivrandon or the threat in Ammardon."

"A third sorcerer?" Mole guessed.

"The third sorcerer," Gion said. "I guessed a long time ago that there would be three. Things in the North seem always to come in threes. Gwarthan and I have scoured the kingdoms since the days of the Hawk Lord in search of the third, to kill him before he came into power. But he has eluded us until now; he has declared himself in the fastness of the island of

Dragonshead in the Mouths of Ystadun. His power is already great, for he is the teacher of the other two sorcerers, a necromancer of the most ancient black order. Storm crows, his spies, his goblins, his mischief-makers have already been seen throughout the kingdoms. Wolfmen have killed crofters in Thrinedor, and travelers through the passes of the Mon Dau into Wild East Pesten have disappeared. And Branddabon is drilling goblins and wildmen even now in the Meads of Crywyll."

"Then it's King Redwen of Crywyll who must challenge Branddabon, not you," Mole said. "That's the law of the kingdoms."

"But Redwen has made no move against the sorcerer," the High King said, "even though Redwen has known about Branddabon longer than we have."

"But that's treachery!" Mole exclaimed. "A breach of your law."

Gion sighed. "It is. Otherwise, Branddabon wouldn't be such a threat. Gwarthan tells me we can crush his power easily if we strike quickly. The problem lies with Redwen himself, who sees my sister's refusal to marry his son as an excuse to escape my authority. I don't think he will fight against us, for he hasn't given up on his son becoming the next High King by marrying Geniolien. But Redwen refuses to help defeat Branddabon unless I betroth Geniolien to his son. But I will bind no one—including you, Moleander—against his will. I won't yield to Redwen's demands. And after I defeat Branddabon, I'll show a little force in the Meads of Crywyll to keep Redwen in step."

"I'll help you defeat Branddabon if you wish," Mole said.

The High King smiled slightly. "No, Moleander. I don't need a confused High Captain. I think I can do without a High Captain in this war, for it will be over soon enough. Go to Aelenwaith. Separate your thoughts. I will keep the High Captaincy vacant until you return."

Standing up, Mole nodded, hesitated, then nodded again. "I have one more favor to ask you before I go," he said.

"Name it."

Mole unfastened the belt of the Sword and laid the weapon on the table. "I won't need this in Aelenwaith," he said.

"I don't think I'll need your Sword against Branddabon," the High King said, watching the sapphires glitter. "And even if I did, I could not use it. It belongs to you, Briarborn."

"Keep it safe for me, then," Mole said, "for I won't take it."

"I will keep it safe," Gion said.

With a last look at the Sword, Mole went to the door. He lingered there, his hand hovering above the latch, his eyes searching the High King's. He frowned, then turned to open the door.

"Good night," he said.

The king looked up. "Good-bye," he said.

Mole closed the door.

· 3 ·

Stone, Fire, and Sea Thunder

IT WAS OPPRESSIVELY hot. The sun glared on the sea. Waves tipped with blinding brightness stretched away to end in a pale line of fire between the water and sky. The afternoon wind, coming from the castle hill, dried the pools of seawater in the rocks and growled against the spray rising from the breakers.

The wind in his hair, Mole stood on the seawall. He listened to the cries of sea birds and the creak of moored fishing boats as he squinted across the water toward a ship anchored in the center of the bay. The hull of the vessel, long and low in the water, was slapped by the waves. A single mast, like a great tree, swung slightly.

"That's the *Taran-y-Mor*," Berrian said from beside Mole, "the last of the twelve ships built by High King Eithodd. King Gion is kind to offer you such a passage."

Mole said nothing, but watched the movement of men on the ship. Two climbed the riggings toward the furled sail. Another dropped over the side of the ship into a boat, which soon separated itself from the *Taran-y-Mor* and edged its way toward the seawall.

"My things are already on board," Mole said. "They need only me, now." He placed the end of the staff in the sand and lowered himself to the beach. Arien jumped down beside him. The breeze pushed her hair into her face.

"I wish you weren't leaving so soon," she said, pushing it away. "You've hardly been back from Taranil a day!"

39

"The sooner I go, the sooner I'll be back."

More people joined Berrian and Merani on the seawall. Ellari moved to one side of Berrian and Gwenith to the other. But Mair dropped down onto the beach and faced Mole.

"I . . . I didn't know you were going," she stammered. "How long will you be gone?"

"Not long," he answered, smiling at her.

Arien tugged at his arm. He turned his head. "You told Fflad farewell, didn't you?"

"This morning. But he hardly understood what I was saying; one of the healing masters had given him an herb brew just before I came. You must promise to take care of him, Arien."

She consented with a dip of her head.

"Mole, Mole," Mair said. "I have a present to give you before you go. I meant to give it to you last night, before the feast, but I couldn't find you." Keeping her eyes on him, she brought from her apron pocket something wrapped in cloth. When she took the cloth away, Mole saw an earthenware goblet, cunningly made, fashioned in the shape of the High King's own ale cup.

"Take it," Mair said. "Please."

He let the staff fall against his shoulder. He held out his hand, but he reconsidered and closed his fist. "No," he said, taking the staff again, "I'd break it on the way to Aelenwaith. Keep it for me until I return."

A scrape on the sand interrupted Mole. Two men climbed from the boat onto the beach. The first, a man in salt-flecked breeches, whom Mole knew to be the captain of the *Taran-y-Mor,* greeted Mole.

"I'm ready," Mole replied. He kissed Arien swiftly on the cheek, slid his hand from hers, then grinned back at the people on the seawall. "Farewell to you all." He started toward the boat, hesitated, then turned back and called to Berrian, "Don't let Ellari drag you back to Thrinedor before I return."

Though Ellari frowned, Berrian laughed. "Good luck, Mole," he said.

Mole stepped into the boat while the two men pushed it from the beach and splashed their way back into it. They nudged the beach away with long oars, then began to row into the bay.

By the time Mole reached the *Taran-y-Mor,* its sail billowed in a freshening wind. A pair of sailors dragged the anchor aboard as Mole climbed in, and waves growling under the hull gave him the sudden impression that the ship was already drifting off.

Putting the ash staff against the bulwarks, Mole took a seat on rigging and nets. The *Taran-y-Mor* turned toward the sea. Mole saw Arien climb onto the seawall and hold up her hand. For a moment the *Taran-y-Mor* seemed motionless, caught in a lull of time, but then the current of the river caught its prow, and the wind filled its sail.

The blue banner of Pesten trailed out over the bow. The sailors shouted to one another above the creak of ropes and the thud of waves. Mole watched the shrinking shore until he saw the people on the dock turn away toward the castle. Only then did he look seaward.

The turquoise face of the sea grew deeper in the distance until it met the sky in a hard, bright line. Mole steadied himself, though the rocking of the ship really didn't bother him. He tasted salt on his lips and felt the hot fingers of the sea wind sort his hair.

After a time, Mole made his way to the bow. He managed to reach the shipmaster without falling, though he had to duck to miss a shift in the sail.

"I hope you like the *Taran-y-Mor*," the shipmaster said, "for you'll find she's the worthiest longship in the kingdoms." He pointed to the prow, which sliced the waves to send up icy spray. "She is swift."

"How long till Aelenwaith?"

"Three days in fair weather, four in foul. We're coming out of the straights now, sir, so unless you're used to the sea, you'd better find a good place to fasten yourself. We're in for some rough water."

Mole reached his seat just as the *Taran-y-Mor* met its first real wave. The ship climbed a rise the size of a hill, then plunged into a trough beyond, breaking with a splash of spray. When Mole looked behind him, he saw the green line of the Pesten shore, broken by a few jagged mountains in the east, vanish behind a great blue wave.

At length the sea flattened again somewhat, and a sailor brought Mole a biscuit and a flask of sun-warmed wine. Mole watched sea birds wing landward over the sail and listened to their cries until they drained into the wash of the sea. He grew sleepy because of the wine and the heat of the movement of the ship, and before he knew what he was doing, he spread his arms on the bulwarks and laid his head on them. He dreamed and woke, dreamed and woke, alternated between the flash of sun and sea and a warm world full of stars. But at last, when the sun grew hot enough that the spray on his arms didn't wake him, he fell asleep.

He woke at sunset to find nothing but grey ocean around him. Thick clouds hid the fall of the sun, and restless waves rolled across the horizon. "I'm afraid we're in for a squall," the shipmaster told Mole. Even as he spoke, a wind shrieked through the sail and sent the royal banner snapping over Mole's head.

Lightning flashed; waves rose, topped with mad foam. The wind drove rain into the ship. A wave struck the bow, tilting the ship backward, almost flinging from the riggings the sailors who were trying to take down the sail. The ship, dwarfed against the clouds, pitched and tossed; and as each wave spun, whirled, swerved, and fell back on itself, timbers groaned. Soon soaked to the skin, Mole clung to the bulwarks, not daring to let go but fearing not to when the waves dragged at him.

The storm continued even when the light failed. Thunder gurgled from the depths and boomed across the sky. Jets of black water washed across Mole's legs. But although the darkness boiled around him, Mole glimpsed a single star above the prow, even before the storm passed away into the north.

Even after Geniolien awoke, she saw fire, heard it hissing against the stones, smelled its smoke. It took her a moment to realize that the fire burning in her grate was not the same fire that had engulfed stone walls in her nightmare. She sighed, suddenly comforted, but the sound of splitting stones continued in her head.

"Dragon fire?" she mused, pressing her blankets to her throat. No, it had been something more real than that. "Goblin fire?" she whispered. "Yes, that was it. Goblin fire. It's been such a long time since I dreamed about the goblin wars. Not since I was a little girl."

Her brother's departure for Crywyll the day before was probably the cause of her nightmare, she realized. Looking at the rain dotting her windows, she hoped Gion had found a dry place to sleep. "Not since I was a *very* little girl," she chided herself. She turned over to face her windows in hope the tap of the rain would lull her back to sleep. But sleep did not come.

* * *

At first Mole thought it was a wave. Next it seemed to be a trick of the sun on the sea. A dimple on the horizon, by noon it grew into a hump, then a green triangle, then, by early afternoon, a great mountain rising out of the sea, topped with a square peak clad in steeply climbing forests.

"The mountain of Aelenwaith!" the shipmaster called out. The wind hurried the *Taran-y-Mor* along the glittering corridor of water toward the island. "The kingdom of Aelenwaith is no more than a heap of sand in the sea. You'll find no treasure there."

Mole laughed. "If my treasure were sand," he said, "I'd have plenty of it. Where is the harbor?"

"On the north side of the island, near a village called Eber Ynys. You can just see it, under that shield-shaped cliff, in the lee of the wind. We'll come there soon, but only long enough to say farewell, for the harbor is shallow, and the High King commands the *Taran-y-Mor* to meet him at Dragonshead."

Mole looked at the island and at the endless water around it. "How am I to return?"

"We will come for you again when our business is done in the west."

"And how long will that be?"

"Two weeks, maybe three," the shipmaster said. Then, reading the disappointment on Mole's face, he added, "But maybe sooner."

Mole looked landward. He soon saw the village the shipmaster had described. It rose on a rocky promontory at the northern tip of the island, stone buildings hugging the cliffs. A recent avalanche had buried the houses nearest the cliffs, and the higher part of the village seemed only a shabby continuance of the mountain. The lower town seemed to belong to the sea, for its houses were stained with salt and seaweed. Wind from the island brought the smell of rotting nets.

"I don't dare go into the harbor with these winds," the shipmaster told Mole. "The waves are coming up. I'll have to let you off on the headland, if you don't mind."

"I don't mind," Mole said. But he rubbed the spray from his arms, watching the waves uneasily.

The ship swung westward to avoid the breakers pushing toward the cliffs, and the sailors adjusted the sail to bring the *Taran-y-Mor* to a glide. Two seamen then raised oars to fend

away the rocks. "I can't get any closer," the shipmaster boomed
to Mole. "You'll have to wet yourself."

With the wind shrieking through the riggings, Mole hesitated. But he glanced at the shipmaster, took the ash staff,
scrambled over the gunwale, and dropped into the sea. Waves
swallowed him to his armpits; ice-cold, they slapped at his
chin. Only the staff kept him from being sucked under the
Taran-y-Mor; he braced it against the hull and pushed himself
away. The _Taran-y-Mor_ rolled at him, golden flanks shim-
mering, but the wind caught its sail and tugged it away from
him. He watched the _Taran-y-Mor_ slip away seaward. Then
he began to swim for the rocks.

Even when he reached shallow water, Mole fought waves
to keep from being dragged under. Foam washed over him,
filling his mouth, and he managed to move landward only by
jabbing the staff into the sand. He was wheezing and dripping
when he reached the rocks, where he collapsed, breathless.

As the sun eased his shivering, warming the back of his neck,
he watched the shell-clad rocks, where a crab scurried. The
odor of salt and rot rose from the pools where the tide had run.
Broken floats, shreds of net, and water-fat planks littered the
rocks on the beach as though a fishing fleet had been driven
onto the shore by a gale.

He stood up a few minutes later and saw two sailless boats
riding the waves in the harbor. It seemed odd to him that in a
town certainly dependent on fishing there should be only two.

Yet the town smelled more intensely of fish than the rocks,
so much so that Mole held his nose before passing the first
cottage. The streets, more strictly the spaces between the houses,
were empty except for a pair of dogs nosing at some refuse.
Glancing back to the sea, Mole saw only a speck of gold in
the direction the _Taran-y-Mor_ had gone. He shivered, hugged
his wet arms, and continued into the village.

He soon saw a stairway that scaled the cliff at the town's
end. A house with several chimneys balanced on the edge of
the cliff, and Mole had just decided that the villagers had gone
there or to the island beyond when he saw a man squatting on
the rocks.

The man seemed to be drawing a net from the breakers. His
clothes were grey and dotted with seawater. They resembled
the town in every respect.

Mole cleared his throat. "Sir—"

The man exploded to his feet, whirling around. Metal glittered in his upraised hand. "Get back, thief! Take no more from me, or your ragtag prince will meet my fish hook!"

Mole leaped back. "I don't mean you any harm!"

Grey eyes burned beneath a mat of mud-colored hair. "Aye, but you've made harm, and you'll pay for your feasting and mocking with your flesh on this hook!"

"I don't mean you any harm!" Mole repeated. Instinctively feeling for his Sword, Mole backed away. "I'm not the one you think I am, whoever that may be. I'm not from this island at all. I've just arrived on a ship from the mainland. Sir, I warn you. Don't be hasty!"

"I don't see any ship, young fool!" the man growled. He moved toward Mole, holding up a hook bigger than his hand.

Mole brought the staff to bear in front of him. "But you see seawater on me. The wind prevented my ship from landing at your harbor. I had to swim ashore."

The man halted, but his eyes remained only slits. "You're a good liar for being one of Good Eiddew's Men."

"Good Eiddew's Men? I don't know what you're talking about. I tell you, I'm not from Aelenwaith. I'm from the mainland, from the other kingdoms. I'm here to look for a woman named Ingra."

"Ingra? I don't know any Ingra. Where did you sail from?"

"Drallm," Mole said. "Ranath Drallm. Four days ago."

The man lowered his hook. An odd light came into his face. "If you came from Drallm, you'll have to prove it to me."

Mole looked down on his clothes. They clung, empty of device or pattern, to his body. "My belongings," he said, setting his jaw, "I left them . . . I left them on the ship!"

"More lies," the man said.

A sound alerted Mole to the house behind him where several men, resembling the first man, gathered. A few women with skinny children watched him, expressionless, from windows.

"I am from Drallm," Mole shouted. "I've come from the mainland, I tell you."

They only looked at him with eyes like stones.

"Wait!" came a shout. "Wait!" Another man broke away from the crowd and strode across the rocks to where Mole stood. Like the others, his eyes were grey, but he was slighter of frame. "Does it occur to you, Eiddew Netmaker, that this man might be telling the truth?"

"Why would he be?"

"In his position, I certainly would," the new man said. He turned to Mole, smiling. "My name is Llawer Smith, and as far as I'm concerned, you're welcome in Eber Ynys, no matter where you come from."

A burly man joined the others. "He hasn't come from Drallm. I've watched the sea all day. And I haven't seen any ship."

"You've scarcely seen your wife, Eiddew the Fisherman," Llawer said, "and you've been married to her for twenty years. If this man says he's come from Drallm, he's come from Drallm. At least we've got to believe him until we find proof otherwise." Llawer glared at Eiddew Netmaker. "It might be a messenger from the High King you almost put on your hook. How would it help our troubles if you had stabbed him?"

"I'm not a messenger from the High King," Mole said. "I'm here in Aelenwaith to find a woman, a kind of relative of mine—"

"More likely you're a spy from Emnos by the look of you," Eiddew the Fisherman interrupted. "The Emnos pirates have ships that come and go quickly, and men that swim from them."

"He can't be from Emnos," Llawer Smith said. "Look at his eyes. They're blue, not brown. He can't be a pirate. Sir," he said to Mole, "you'd better come back to my smithy and stand by the forge, or you'll catch your death in this wind." Mole started after Llawer, but a thick hand on his shoulder stopped him.

"You'll regret taking him to your house if he's one of the pirates or a new member of Good Eiddew's Men," Eiddew Netmaker said. "No good will come of him, mark my words."

"If we marked your words," Llawer retorted, "we'd all die of despair. I'll admit he isn't the messenger from the High King we'd all hoped for, but he isn't a thief, either."

Mole faced Llawer. "You're expecting a messenger from the High King?"

"A messenger at least." Llawer's smile faded. "You're from Drallm. The High King certainly got our plea for help, didn't he?"

"Plea for help?" Mole pondered. "No, I don't think so."

"But we sent a letter with a shipmaster in the spring," Llawer said. "The shipmaster promised to deliver it. We haven't heard anything since, all these months. I thought at first you might be—"

"I don't think your letter ever got to Drallm," Mole said. Looking at the staff thoughtfully, he felt the eyes of the townspeople on him. "And a ship from here sank in a spring tempest, or at least it didn't return to the harbor at Drallm."

"I knew it!" Eiddew Netmaker cried out. "I knew it! Our letter never even reached the High King. No help will come. Not from the High King, not from his servants, not from anyone! All we will get are thieves and pirates, like this one."

"When I return to Drallm," Mole said, looking at the people, "I'll take a message to the High King myself—"

Eiddew the Fisherman bared his teeth. Mole saw some of the other village men close around him. He looked to Llawer. "You'd better come with me," the smith said, "now."

Llawer took Mole in the crook of his arm and ushered him away from the other men, who closed in behind him. "Don't look back," Llawer whispered as they passed the first house. But Mole couldn't help seeing the other men bunch around Eiddew Netmaker. The women hung back in the doorways when he approached, and the children hid their faces. Mole heard footfalls—many of them, slow and deliberate—behind him.

Llawer turned down a narrow alley where he hurried Mole to a low door at the end, pushed him in, and turned around. The men of the town gathered in the far end of the alley.

"Go home, all of you," Llawer shouted. "You're like Good Eiddew's Men yourselves, turning into a mob for nothing. Go home!" For a moment it seemed that the crowd would not break, but one by one the men drifted away. Eiddew Netmaker was the last to go.

When Llawer stepped inside, Mole began to shiver. "Thank you," he said.

"Stand by the forge," Llawer said, "or the cold will kill you."

Through the cracks in the stone and iron fittings, orange coals glowed in the forge. Their light dappled the low ceiling and Mole's hands when he put them over it. He could smell iron dust and coal, now, more than fish; and the light from the forge revealed walls hung with hammers, scythes, blades, and hooks, some the size of the one Eiddew Netmaker had used to threaten Mole.

"Now that I've saved your life—twice," Llawer said, "you might at least tell me your name."

"I am Moleander of Ranath Drallm." The coals hissed when seawater dripped from his sleeve.

"And you've come in search of a lost relative?"

"Yes. Exactly." Mole looked up. "And I don't much like being threatened when I've done no harm. Are people always so friendly in Aelenwaith? I've found better receptions in the wild lands of Vivrandon!"

"Ah, but you don't understand, Moleander. The people of Eber Ynys haven't always been like this, and they wouldn't be, if it wasn't for our troubles. Not that I think Eiddew Netmaker had any right to come at you with a hook. But I know the frustration he feels."

"Why? What's so wrong here?" Mole remembered the planks he had seen among the rocks. "Has a storm wrecked your fishing fleet?"

"Yes," Llawer said, moving around the forge, "but that's just the beginning."

"Tell me more."

"As you guessed, almost all our boats were beaten to splinters in the last storm. That's because the Emnos pirates burned our docks and ship moorings in a raid at high summer. Now no ships can harbor at Aelenwaith. And without our fishing boats, we starve."

"But surely you have fields and orchards higher on the island."

"We did once," Llawer replied, "but they aren't any good to us now, for the woods between here and there are full of boars and mountain cats. A boar gored a child only last month in the apple orchard. And two days ago, the earth shook and rocks from the cliff fell to bury half the town."

Mole licked his lips. "Don't you have a king? You send to the High King for help, but you should know he's busy enough holding the realm together. A new sorcerer has arisen. What about your own king, the king of Aelenwaith?"

Llawer's brows fell until they nearly touched his eyelids. "The king," he answered, "is one of our greatest troubles. The old king died almost five years ago, leaving his son, Prince Eiddew VII, to the throne. The reason there are so many Eiddews, by the way, is because Eiddew was the name of the founder of this kingdom. Prince Eiddew is his heir. Boy kings can be good, as High King Gion was; but some remain boys, not kings. Eiddew and a group of other young men, who call themselves Good Eiddew's Men, live in Clifftop House in a continual state of merrymaking. They love to hunt and roast what they kill, so every week one of our cows or pigs is missing. Not many are left."

Mole moved to the door. In the alley bits of net stirred in the sea wind. "With Aelenwaith in a wreck, how will I find her?" he said, more to himself than to Llawer.

"What's her name?"

"Ingra," Mole said, thinking of Arien. "Lady Ingra."

Llawer looked at his forge for a long time, then shrugged. "The name seems familiar, but I don't know the woman."

Mole sighed and looked into the alley again.

"You can stay with me while you're in Aelenwaith," Llawer said. "I'll give you what help I can, but I can't say what help you'll get from anyone else in Eber Ynys. And I hope you can stomach dried herring."

Raising an eyebrow in question, Mole turned around.

Llawer forced a smile. "That's all I have."

Flies buzzed against the window of the Library of Bards. Beyond the glass, bees lifted and circled above the rosebushes. A stroke of pale sunlight fell from the windows on a dusty table, a stack of books, and the hands of Princess Geniolien. The princess, quill locked in her teeth, read a line, scribbled something on a curl of parchment, then snapped the book shut. She turned around. "Any more?" she asked.

Standing on a stool with an armload of books, Merani nodded. "That stack by your inkpot," she said.

Geniolien took the top book and opened it. "This isn't one," she said in a moment. "Merani, this one's a poem about a Crywyll king."

"It can't be," Merani said, reddening a little. "I'm sure I've found only books of enchantment for you. In fact, I think that one even said 'magic' in big letters on the front page."

"It says, 'Madric,' not 'magic,'" Geniolien said. "That was the king's name, I suppose." She laid the book aside and opened another.

Merani stepped down from the stool. "I'm sorry. Geniolien, but I'm starting to see the word *magic* in my dreams! We've been at this so long, looking through all these dusty old chronicles. And you still haven't found what you're looking for." Merani moved up behind Geniolien, who was thumbing through a volume of minor spells. "And why won't you let me help you more than by finding books for you? I mean, I know about more things than just hawks and arrows. I was born in Fell-heath, the most magical place in the kingdoms, the place where all the wizards were born. My grandmother was an enchantress. Why won't you tell me what you're looking for?"

"Because I don't *know* what I'm looking for," Geniolien said. "I'm not looking for any particular spell or any particular person. I'm looking for a notion, a *feeling—*"

"Then tell me about your feeling."

"I already have," Geniolien said, blowing the dust from the next book, "several times."

"Your dreams?" Merani guessed. "But what do nightmares about something that happened all those years ago have to do with this?"

"What, indeed," Geniolien said. "I don't know, actually. I'll tell you when I find out."

"You know more than you're telling me," Merani countered. "Listen, Geniolien. If you don't tell me more, I won't be able to help you any more. Tell me about your dream again, then tell me what you're looking for."

Geniolien reclined in her chair. "All right. But you must promise that you won't think me mad—"

"I think you're mad already. You've got to prove to me that you're not."

"When I was very young," Geniolien said, "not more than one or two, the goblin wars reached the walls of Drallm. There had been goblin wars farther north for years, and my father, High King Eithodd, died fighting in one in the marshes. I don't even remember him. But I do remember my mother, High Queen Gien. I remember how tightly she held me the morning Gion went off to fight the goblins. Gion was only a boy then, hardly old enough to hold a sword. From outside there came sounds of shouts and flames and thunder. The thunder was the worst, though it really wasn't thunder at all—it was goblin fire powder being lit under the walls. Then I heard stones falling, and my mother cried out that the goblins had blasted a gap in the wall and were coming through it. She ran, carrying me in her arms. Her hair covered my face, and an awful rumbling chased us. I don't recall anything that happened after that, but I think my brother and his men managed to drive the goblins back through the gap. They've never blasted the walls again, though I've often dreamed of it since."

"Dreams are dreams," Merani said. "You don't need to worry, Geniolien. We aren't being besieged now."

"*I* am," Geniolien said. "I've dreamed of fire powder and falling stones every night since Gion left for Crywyll. I hear thunder in the darkness. And last night I dreamed about Gion. He was standing against a wall with fear in his eyes, as if something had cornered him there. Then thunder began and black flames came up through the wall. Gion threw up his hands. He cried out, but the stones covered him."

Merani touched Geniolien's arm. "You don't need a spell," she said, "you need your brother. His leaving stirred up some old nightmares, that's all. Didn't you say that when you were a child, he left just before the goblins started blasting the walls?"

Geniolien considered, but only for a moment. "But it isn't just a nightmare, Merani. What happened when I was a little girl was real. It can happen again. Only this time there won't be anybody to stop the goblins in the gap."

Merani swallowed. "But there aren't any goblins here now."

"Oh no? Captain Berrian saw some by the river last night."

"Captain Berrian," Merani said, "is trying to find an excuse—any excuse—to keep Ellari from dragging him back to Thrinedor. Besides, if any goblin gets over the wall, he'll have to meet my arrows before he gets to you. And your brother will be back from Crywyll in another week or so. Then everything will be all right again."

Glass-eyed, Geniolien stared at the roses beyond the window. "Find some more books, Merani," she said.

• 4 •

Threat of Red Dawn

THREE DAYS PASSED, and the wind off the sea did not stop. But it did little to ease the heat, and as Mole roamed among the houses of Eber Ynys, he began to think he was turning into seaweed and fire. For three days he had exchanged no word with any of the townspeople except Llawer; they shunned him, peering at him with empty eyes from behind their curtains. Once a child had thrown a stone at him, and once a young girl had laughed at him. Once Mole had cornered an old woman in Llawer's alley, but she said nothing to him, though her eyes lit at the mention of Lady Ingra.

"I'll never find Ingra, even if she is here," Mole said to Llawer on the morning of the fourth day. The smith wiped his hands across his apron and tossed more wood chips into his blaze. But he did not smile. "I will fail in what I came here to do because your people won't help me."

Llawer looked at him. "Have you ever thought," he said, "that the reason they won't help you is because you won't help them?"

Mole blinked. "I don't know what you mean."

"Don't you?" Llawer took his tongs in his hands. "Last night you told me why you had come here, to search for the parents of your friends in hope that you could find your own. You told me something your old guardian said, something about searching for others to find yourself. Have you forgotten so soon?"

Mole dropped his head; he felt his fingers tighten around the staff. "I guess I had forgotten it," he said.

Llawer made no reply. Instead, he began to pump the bellows. The coals hissed and reddened as he put a strip of iron on the anvil. Glancing at Mole, he took up a hammer and began to beat the iron with slow, even strokes.

Mole watched Llawer's soot-smudged arm rise and fall. Then he moved to the door of the smithy.

"Moleander," Llawer said, "you're going to the village again?"

"No, I'm going to Clifftop House."

The hint of a smile crossed Llawer's lips. "Clifftop House? Why?"

"The prince of Aelenwaith is Eber Ynys's greatest problem. And though I can't stop earthquakes or resurrect fishing fleets, I can take care of princes. I've dealt with princes before."

Grinning, Llawer laid down his hammer. "I'm going with you, then."

"No," Mole said. "I want to go alone. Besides, I want you to do something for me while I'm gone. I want you to gather as many of the people as you can. Bring them to the foot of the stairway."

"That much I'll do gladly," Llawer said. "But you can't challenge all of Good Eiddew's Men by yourself. It's dangerous!"

"Very dangerous," Mole said, "for Good Eiddew and his men."

At first the ancient stair in the cliffs was so crumbled that Mole could scarcely climb it, and he had to use the staff to cross the rubble. But higher up the steps were as cleanly hewn as if they had been cut into the cliff only the day before. Mole fairly bounded up them. Eber Ynys shrunk away below him until the whole town seemed no more than a stack of squarish rocks.

From the first trees, the slopes of Aelenwaith ran up to meet the sky. After the fish-smelling town, the scents of weeds and leaves and bark seemed strange to Mole as he hurried along a grass-choked path across a yard filled with trees. Clifftop House seemed to have been built at the same time as the town, because it was cut of the same stone and shingled with the same wood. Several heavy doors, all shut, waited in the shadows of the trees, and chimneys, at least seven of them, pricked above the roof of leaves. Smoke trailed into the sky from the lowest chimney. Mole smelled roasting beef before he was even near the house.

He leaped onto the steps of the nearest door and rapped on it three times with the staff. A sound of voices came from within; one, particularly high-pitched, seemed to be approaching the door. Mole darted aside and pressed himself against the doorframe.

The door opened, and a narrow face poked out. "Who's there?" A boy stepped onto the porch, licking gravy from his lips. "Who's there, I say!"

Mole clenched his teeth, then flew at the boy, hooking the staff around his neck. The boy squeaked, kicking as Mole pulled him against his shoulder. "Who is it?" the boy said, trying to wriggle from Mole's stranglehold. "Let me go!"

Mole kicked the door open and shoved the boy before him into a crowded, smoke-filled common room. On a spit over the fire, a side of beef sizzled, and because someone had no knowledge of flues, a haze hung in the beams of the ceiling. Oddments of various kinds, swords, bones, broken casks, and shards of glass littered the room, and on the table lay a disarray of meat platters and empty ale flagons. Half a dozen young men crouched around the table. Two more squatted by the fire, catching drippings from the meat with their fingers. All of them shouted and laughed until the sunlight from the door struck them.

One by one they looked at Mole. Mole sent his captive sprawling to the floor, then he strode to the table. Pushing his arms under it, he heaved it on its side. Platters crashed, beef flew, and bottles shattered. One of the men stood up, but Mole pushed him back into his chair with the staff. But three more sprang up before Mole could turn around. One snatched his staff, and the others grasped his arms. Mole shook them away, but more caught him, throwing their weight against him to keep him from thrashing them off.

The taller of the two men by the fire, a man wearing a silver brooch, stood up. He glowered at Mole. "Rogue! Who are you to break in on our feast? You'll soon curse the day you dared touch Eiddew's feasting table!"

"He may curse the day soon," one of the boys at Mole's arm growled, "but right now, he's getting away. Madring,

Cendwn, don't just stand there. Come here! Come here and help us hold him."

"You'll need more than feast-fat boys to hold me," Mole said, seizing the man by the fire. "And if you're Prince Eiddew, you'd better thank your luck these boys are here to protect you."

Prince Eiddew's hand went to his sword. He stepped forward. "I am *King* Eiddew," he said. "And you'd better thank *your* luck that my men are here to hold you, or you would have met my sword a moment ago. Who are you?"

Heaving his arms backward, Mole shook himself away. The boys came toward him again, but Prince Eiddew commanded them away. "Answer me!" he thundered to Mole. "Now!"

"My name is Moleander," he said, eyes burning.

"And who is Moleander?" Prince Eiddew sneered. "I've heard of no such man." He examined Mole, then added, "If he is a man at all."

"Moleander is a searcher," Mole returned. "And sometimes he is an avenger. He is one who is concerned about a princeling who hides in his father's mansion to feast with hungry fools while his people starve. He is one angry with a young prince who slaughters his own people's livestock for sport, who watches them waste away in despair!"

"You're meddling in what's not your business, then."

"I know what he is!" the boys beside Prince Eiddew shouted. "He's a do-gooder!"

Prince Eiddew's knuckles went white with rage. "He's a boy fresh from his mother's cooking fire, come to preach about error in the house of a king! Now, Moleander. Let me introduce *myself*. I am a king who doesn't like his food strewn on the floor and his friends wrestled. I'm a man who dislikes common fools and meddlers. I am the best swordsman in Aelenwaith, and anyone who does wrong to me must answer to my sword."

"Those who live by the sword die by it," Mole said. "I don't carry one."

"Milksop! I'll lend you one."

Flexing his fingers, Mole nodded slowly.

At Prince Eiddew's command, one of the men unsheathed his sword and handed it to Mole. The blade seemed heavy to Mole after the easy balance of Sodrith, but after only a few turns of his wrist, the weapon became part of him.

The boys dragged the table to one side of the room and pushed debris away with their feet. Meanwhile Prince Eiddew shed his tunic and tested his jeweled sword. Mole watched him twirl the blade, carefully noting the flaws in his movement. Shaking his hair back, Prince Eiddew pretended to turn around, but suddenly he whirled, lunged and drove the sword toward Mole's chest.

Mole barely managed to leap aside. He parried the second blow, and with a third of his own, he sent Prince Eiddew's sword flying. Hooking his fingers into his belt, he lowered the sword.

"I . . . I wasn't ready," Prince Eiddew stammered. He crawled under the table to retrieve his weapon. "I . . . I forgot to tell you that on Aelenwaith the man who has been insulted has the right to fight with a comrade against the person who accused him."

"I will fight two," Mole said.

Prince Eiddew picked the brawniest of his comrades.

When Prince Eiddew began to bout anew, Mole blocked him with a sweep and a twist, knocked the second warrior to the floor with his flat, then sent Prince Eiddew's blade under the table again. But this time Mole kept his sword up. Holding the other man down with his foot, Mole drove Prince Eiddew back against the wall, where he held him with the sword at his throat.

Prince Eiddew slid to the floor. "Slay me, demon, slay me!"

"I don't have any intention of killing you, Prince Eiddew. I didn't want even to fight you. But some people seem to learn lessons only from swords." Mole faced the others. "Do any of the rest of you need a quick lesson?"

Wide eyes told him no one did. Mole shrugged, rubbed the flat of the sword on his tunic, then returned it to its owner, who took it from a distance. Prince Eiddew, when he crept up from the floor, seemed stunned.

His face softened. "What is your lesson?" he asked.

"Not such a hard one to learn," Mole said, "but a difficult one to practice. So before you begin, I want you all to take an oath."

"We won't make any promises!" someone said.

"You will make—*and keep*—all the promises I ask you to," Mole said, "or you'll have to fight me—"

"And me," Prince Eiddew said suddenly. He bit his lip as

he brushed himself off. "Any of you who don't do what this man says will have to fight me, too. And I'm the second best swordsman in Aelenwaith. Something you said, Moleander, something you said . . . reminded me of my father." For a moment Eiddew bent his head and his shoulders slumped; but then he looked at Mole, eyes glittering. "Ask what you want. All of us will obey."

"I'm not asking you to promise for my sake," Mole said. "I'm asking you to promise for the sake of the people of Aelenwaith. You won't kill any more of their cattle and pigs, and you will come back to Eber Ynys with me to repair as much of your mischief as you can."

Eiddew squared his shoulders. "We will all promise that much," he said. "You have the word of a prince."

"You mean," Mole corrected, "the word of a king."

Eiddew looked at the floor.

"Wait a minute!" someone shouted. "This is all very noble, but we hunt to eat. What will we do for meat?"

"Hunting tame animals," Mole said, "is like shooting arrows at corn! If you want good meat and good hunting, there is a herd of wild boars in the woods between here and the orchards. No one will mind if you roast one or two of them."

"But . . ." the boy who had answered the door said, "the boars are—"

"Dangerous?" Mole finished. "That depends on which is fiercer, the hunted or the hunter."

"Personally," another boy ventured, "I thought all along that hunting those boars would be fun. I dare say if we sport them, they'll scatter all over the island, and then we'll make real hunting out of it. No boar's too big or fast for Good Eiddew's Men, is it, boys?" Several of them nodded in agreement.

"I'm glad you aren't afraid of boars," Mole said, "because I want all of you to go to the orchards now. Gather as much fruit as you can carry, then bring it and your beef and your ale to the village. There will be a feast in Ynys tonight."

"Go," Eiddew commanded. "Quickly!"

After they had gone, Eiddew stumbled into a chair and buried his face in his hands. Mole, taking the staff quietly in his hands, waited for Eiddew to speak. In a few moments Eiddew raised his head. "Can I tell you something?"

Mole took a chair beside the prince.

"My father . . . my father was a great swordsman, like you. I asked him once how he'd become so good. He told me that whenever he met a better warrior, he took that warrior's advice. You are the better man. I will believe what you say. I've done something wrong—very wrong—and I don't even know how it all began or what I can do to right it."

"All roads lead two ways," Mole replied. He glanced out the windows toward the blue of the sea beyond the maples. "And your road back lies through Eber Ynys."

"I understand," Eiddew said. He followed Mole to the door.

From the top of the cliff stair, Mole saw that Llawer Smith had gathered the people in the village square. Partway down the steps, Mole heard their murmur. From the foot of the cliff, Mole saw Llawer Smith and Eiddew Netmaker facing one another on a doorstep, shaking red fists and shouting. It seemed that most of the town sided with Eiddew Netmaker, for whenever Llawer spoke, the crowd began to shout and hiss.

Their noise ended, however, when Prince Eiddew pushed his way through them to the doorstep. Mole could not force his way through the crowd because they backed away from the prince. A child cried out. A woman hushed him. Both Llawer Smith and Eiddew Netmaker withdrew from the porch. The crowd's silence, at first tense, soon became hushed and expectant.

Prince Eiddew stepped forward. He went red, then pale, then red again. At last he managed to say, "I'm sorry."

"Sorry!" someone cried out. A new murmur rose.

"Will your being sorry bring back our dead cattle?" Eiddew Netmaker shouted, "or mend our nets?"

"Or feed our children?" a woman added.

Spreading his arms to the crowd, Prince Eiddew opened his mouth, but no words came. More of the villagers began to shout until the uproar drove Prince Eiddew back against the house.

"Wait!" Mole bellowed. "All of you wait!" He plowed his way to the doorstep and took a stance in front of Prince Eiddew. With the staff he barred several of the townsmen, Eiddew Netmaker among them, who tried to reach the prince. "Listen, all of you! Listen to me!" The crowd, however, continued to shout; some of the men near the steps began stooping for stones. Incensed, Mole shoved Eiddew Netmaker back with his staff, climbed the stairs, and screamed out, "Listen!"

The hubbub, very suddenly, melted away.

"Are you deaf?" Mole said. "Did you hear what your king said?" He glared at the crowd. "Of course being sorry won't change what's happened. I know that. But what he hasn't said—what you haven't let him say—is what he has promised to do to make amends."

"Yes," Prince Eiddew said, coming forward. "I won't kill your cattle, and my men will hunt wild boars as meat for your tables, until the herds can grow again. And I'll clear the orchards of wild animals, so your children can pick fruit there." Prince Eiddew glanced at Mole. "I don't expect all of you to forgive me yet. But give me a chance to prove my good will!"

"Words, words, words!" Eiddew Netmaker scowled. "We've heard words from your kind before. We can't eat promises, no matter how sweet they are. We can't eat words!"

A hush fell but broke a moment later when Llawer Smith laughed. All heads turned to him, but he chuckled again, pointing to Eiddew Netmaker. "I've been waiting for years to make a fool out of you, Netmaker, but at last you've done it yourself, with no help from me at all!"

Someone else laughed, a woman from the back of the crowd.

Soon the whole crowd began laughing, for Good Eiddew's Men had come into the square. Most of them carried baskets brimming with apples and pears. Two of them shouldered a spitted side of beef. Each of the last three carried a keg of ale, which they stood in front of the steps where Prince Eiddew had spoken.

"Here," he said, "are words you can eat. I meant what I said. I promise you that all Aelenwaith's food will be yours. And for tonight at least, let's eat and drink and forget our problems. Let's have a feast. Well, what are you waiting for? Bring out your tables, your crockery. You boys, get her driftwood for a bonfire." Before Prince Eiddew had finished, tables ringed the square, and children darted to and fro among them, apple cores in their hands. The men of the town, all except Eiddew Netmaker, drank ale as they set fire to the heap of wood the village boys collected. At twilight someone brought out a harp and someone a long flute; some men and women danced in the firelight. Others ate and talked and laughed.

Sitting on a porch, Mole could scarcely believe that the townspeople he now watched were the same ones who had met him on the rocks and watched him from their doorways. Yet he still felt removed from them, and he shivered in spite of the bonfire. His gaze wandered from the feast to the stars, faint behind the rising smoke from the fire.

"Moleander?"

Startled, Mole looked up at Llawer Smith.

"Moleander, I've been looking for you everywhere. I've been meaning to thank you . . . to tell you that you were right when you said you knew about princes—"

"Not princes exactly," Mole said, "pretenders. Most princes are pretenders, you know, but then again, so are most people at one time or another."

Llawer looked toward the feast. "I knew you could help us the moment I saw you."

"This," Mole said with a sweep of his hand, "is the ale's work, not mine. It will wear off in the morning, and I think your friends will like me less then than they do now."

"What do you mean?"

"You've asked me to help you," Mole said, "and I intend to do just that. But this feast has only put off your problems, no matter how pleasant it is. The real work begins tomorrow."

Llawer scratched his side in contemplation. "And what about your own task here? What about your search for Lady Ingra?"

Mole looked at the stars again. "It must wait," he said.

Prince Eiddew called the people together in the town square an hour before noon. Ashes from the previous night's fire still steamed into the sea breeze, and half-full ale cups caught the sun's light. King Eiddew painstakingly explained the plan that he, Moleander, and Llawer Smith had devised earlier that morning; and when he finished, Mole spoke to quell the few murmurs of disagreement.

"Prince Eiddew has given you a feast, a promise, and a plan," Mole said, "and he has offered everything he has to help you. The least you can do in return is to offer your obedience."

The first task began after the noon meal. Mole himself strained to lift the first stone from the rubble under the cliffs. Lugging it out onto the rocks, he heaved it into the sea in a shallow place that he and Eiddew Fisherman had discovered at dawn. Together Llawer Smith and Prince Eiddew brought the next boulder, half a dozen children the next. The women carried smaller rocks in baskets. It was hot work, and the sea swallowed the stones they threw into it while the mountain tumbled more down upon them.

Evening laid shadows deèp on the mountain and on the sea. Good Eiddew's Men brought a boar from the uplands and roasted it in the town square. But though the people ate, none of them celebrated, and the lights soon emptied from their windows. Mole had intended to walk the rocks in order to study the progress of the work, but he found himself stumbling to his cot in Llawer's smithy.

Two weeks dragged by before the seawall rose on the rocks and a breakwater extended into the bay. The houses by the cliffs, newly cleared and rebuilt, housed the new shipworks to be managed by Eiddew the Fisherman; Good Eiddew's Men promised to cut pines from the top of the mountain for the Fisherman's men to fit into new fishing boats.

In spite of his weariness, Mole couldn't help but smile over the glass-smooth harbor. "I like your new dike," he told Prince Eiddew, who stood beside him. "Wherever did you find it?"

Eiddew smiled. "Mole, I've got an idea. But you must tell me if it's a good one, because you're from the mainland. You know what's proper for kings to do. I'm thinking of leaving Clifftop House—we can turn it into a storehouse or something. But I don't want to live there any more. It makes me feel . . . too royal."

"That sounds like something Berrian told me once," Mole said, "about being crown prince." Eiddew did not seem to hear.

"I think I'll build a house here in Ynys. I could bring the flowerboxes and the draperies and the shutters down from Clifftop House and distribute them—this town is so grey, it looks like part of the cliff. But what do you think about abandoning Clifftop House. Is it proper?"

"If it isn't," Mole said, "it ought to be."

Mole saw King Eiddew, as he was thenceforth called, bargaining for a lot of land with Morafin Landmaster the next day.

One bright morning when he returned from working general repair on the harbor front, Mole found Llawer washing the walls of his smithy. Llawer whistled the same tune the harpist had played at the first feast until he saw Mole appear. "I've got news for you, Moleander. First of all, have you heard about the baby the wife of Eiddew the Tailor delivered last night?"

"It was a boy, wasn't it?"

"Yes, and Eiddew wants to name him after you." Llawer licked his lips as he watched Mole's expression. "If you stay in Aelenwaith much longer, your name might become as popular as Eiddew."

Mole chuckled. "May the Emperor forbid that!"

"The other half of my news is a little stranger," Llawer resumed, "and it, *she*, rather, is waiting for you around the end of the alley, on the seaward side. She came here earlier this morning, asking for you, and when I told her you were gone, she said she'd wait there. She wouldn't stay here."

"Who is it?"

"A woman who's lived in Ynys for as long as I can remember. But it's funny, I don't know her name. I don't think anybody does."

"Do you think that it's—I mean, could it be"—Mole felt his cheeks fade—"Lady Ingra?"

"Some searches take care of themselves," Llawer said.

Bolting away from the door, Mole fairly ran down the alley. When he reached the street, he looked in one direction and then another, but saw only sunshine on stones and the sea beyond. But just as he had chosen a direction to search, he saw a bent, black-robed woman in the shade of the nearest house.

But his throat tightened, for he knew at once she couldn't be Arien's mother. Her iron-colored hair frayed from her patched cowl. Her face was lean, bent inward, so netted with wrinkles that Mole could scarcely make out her features. Her body, surely as age-twisted as her hands, lost itself in an oversized cloak stained and stitched alternately. Mole recognized the woman as the one who had avoided his questioning in the smith's alley a few weeks before.

"What do you want?" he said, stiffening.

"You emptied my house of rocks and patched my roof," she said. "And I was taught as a very little girl to repay a favor with a favor."

"Lady Ingra," Mole breathed, "you know where she is?"

"Let me say that I know where she isn't," the woman said. She fixed her eyes on Mole. "She never lived in Ynys, my boy. I haven't seen her for almost seventeen years now, not since she came here to see her husband off to Pesten. She's never come back, and neither has he. I don't think anybody even remembers them now but me. The old king did. But he's dead, of course."

"But what about Ingra? If she didn't live in Ynys, where did she live? At Clifftop House?"

The woman smiled a little. "Oh, no. Her husband came from a very old family who had a house farther up the mountain, in the tall trees. They never came to Ynys much, even before Lord Escandrin left us. It is said they had their own ships in a secret cove."

"Where is this house?" Mole demanded.

The old woman gave him directions, but Mole hardly heard the last of them. He dashed away toward the stairs. "But I doubt you'll find her still there!" the old woman called after him.

He passed up the cliff stair into the meadows. Clifftop House fell behind him as he found the cow trail the woman had spoken of. He followed it through the trees. The orchards faded behind them, and he soon climbed into a forest of tall, leafy trees free of undergrowth, where slices of sunlight streamed onto fallen logs. He passed the place where he had helped Eiddew the Fisherman cut timbers for new ships; he passed the clearing where Good Eiddew's Men had killed their first boar. Then, after what seemed an hour of running, he came to the house.

It was longer than Clifftop House and made of dark wood and white plaster. Thick weeds overgrew the path to its door, and the branches of the trees hid its roof.

Although he expected no answer, he knocked at the door. The windows of the house, rust-colored with dust, stared at him emptily. The click of weeds against the walls of the house when the breeze stirred them spoke of long hours of silence, long years of quiet.

He pushed the door open. Dust clouded up, blinding him. Coughing, he moved in and found himself in a room that reminded him of the High King's chambers because of its oak paneling and high ceiling. Dust lay thick on the floor, on tables and chairs scattered around the room, on a wooden stair leading upward. It was obvious that no one had been in the house for many years; not even the faintest footprint appeared in the dust. Yet although he knew Ingra could not still be in the house, he hesitated, touching almost absently one of the dust-hidden humps on a table. The print of his finger revealed a letter of pen-script on a parchment page, so he brushed more dust away, enough to find that it was a book opened to its first page. The message in the book was not an easy script to read, so Mole muttered it aloud to himself:

"Escandrin. These words are for you, should you return to this house. I received a letter from the mainland saying that you and the children were missing. I have gone with Eiren to look for you, and I will not come back until I have found you. All of you. If chance has brought you, Ingradd, and Ielyn back to the island, watch for me under the stars and look for me when dawn comes." The dust stung Mole's eyes so he could make out no more than the final words, "Your Ingra."

Wind from the door turned the page in Mole's hand, and he saw that Ingra had written her message in a volume of poems by Cyranus. Turning around, Mole saw that the wind had scattered the dust from an object near the door, something cased in carefully embroidered linen. When Mole lifted the cloth away, he found a harp whose strings, though broken, still hummed in the breeze from the door.

Mole left the house, pulling the door shut behind him. With him he took only the book; he tucked it in the breast of his tunic as he waded through the weeds. At the edge of the trees he turned back to look at the house. And suddenly he knew that both Escandrin and Ingra, like the house, lay under the quiet shiftings of wind and leaves. Yet he knew also that he had found Fflad and Arien's parents—the harp and the book were proof enough of that.

He didn't follow the path back to the cliff stair. Instead he wandered among the trees, touching their smooth bark, wending his way toward the sea. He began to wonder about his own parents, if he would ever find them, if he had ever passed their graves or their home without knowing it, if they, as Ingra, had searched for him. He came to the sea cliffs and walked along them, with the sound of spray far below. He smelled foam on the rocks. Closing his eyes, he breathed the sea wind deeply.

Smoke. He opened his eyes. Not wood smoke but an oily smoke that brought to mind a dozen vivid pictures of burning. He halted, and from the forest and the sea, came tendrils of vapor curling over the ancient cliffs, rising in the direction of Eber Ynys.

Arien coughed thickly at the smoke from her fire, but she kept close to it all the same. For she was cold. The foggy summer-autumn night sent fingers of mist under her door and choked the blaze in her grate, making it small and purple. It was hard to imagine that King Gion was overdue from Crywyll, and not more than a handful of warriors were left to guard the castle. Everyone had been seeing goblins in every shadow! If only Mole hadn't gone off treasure hunting!

She glanced at the web of red light and brown shadows the fire made of her room. "If Mole gets himself killed in Aelenwaith," she said aloud, "I'll never forgive him. I haven't forgiven him yet for what happened at Rathvidrian, because it was only by the power of Amreth—"

Her last words seemed to echo in the fireplace. "The power of Amreth," the flames seemed to whisper. "The power of Amreth," the stones seemed to mutter. Arien sprang from her stool, backing away from the fire. There was a sudden heat in her room. It began to make her drowsy, to make her see shapes in the fire, yet it gripped her with enormous and terrifying strength.

And like the fire, it continued to grow.

"No!" she shrieked, then she whispered, "No! Not yet."

She knew the voice that spoke next; it was that of Rhea, Lady Fellflood, who spoke as if through the flames in the grate. "Mountainflower. Your time is coming."

Arien clutched her throat. "No, Rhea. It can't." She seemed to see tiny gold blossoms in the fire. "It can't," she repeated.

"It can. And it will. Very soon. It is beginning, even now."

Arien felt it. It was something like a wind inside her, strengthening her limbs, smoothing the creases on her forehead, touching her mind with fire.

The flames retreated into the grate again, but Arien stood away from it, fists clenched. "No," she said, but her voice was calm and even. She had known it would come; she had always known it would come. And she needed it. She needed its strength. But not too soon.

"Mole!" she cried out. "Mole! Where are you when I need you?"

The darkness folded around to comfort her.

Bursting through the last line of trees, Mole saw smoke flooding up over the cliff. Only one thing could be burning— Eber Ynys.

Mole saw it all when he reached the brink of the stair.

Through the smoke he saw flames licking the roofs. Sounds of battle—the clash of weapons and cries of anguish—rang out over the sea. As Mole rushed down the steps, he wondered who had attacked the town. But he soon knew, for in the harbor, two long ships waited. Twice the size of the *Taran-y-Mor*, each ship had two masts hung with red sails and black banners. Armored men boiled from the sides of the ships to the rocks, where Mole saw the men of Eber Ynys making a stand.

Pirates. Outlaws of the sea and their black ships from Emnos.

Mole found women and children bunching against the cliffs. "Fly!" he cried out to them. He hardly dared slow down to warn them. "Run! Up the stairs! Scatter into the island!" Mole had no time to see if they obeyed, for droves of pirates were coming ashore, to be contained by a frail line of Aelenwaith men. A glimpse of a fallen pirate told Mole that the men of Emnos were fierce people, broad, swarthy, well-armored, and well-trained. Against such numbers of them, hope seemed beyond reason. Mole had fought enough campaigns to know that. But he took up a blade from the fallen man and ran toward the beach.

"Rally!" Mole yelled when he saw the Aelenwaith men falling back. He looked for King Eiddew and Llawer Smith, but if they were on the rocks, he could not see them. Leaping from the seawall into the breakers, Mole thrust up the sword as a standard and cried out, "Forward!" At first none of the townsmen seemed to hear him. Armed only with short swords and a few bows, they fell back against the houses.

"Drive them into the sea!" Mole shouted. "It's our only hope!" He tried to yell more, but a stinging blow across his shoulder silenced him. He spun around, charged, and drove his blade down into the throat of an enemy. In a frenzy, he withdrew it, thrust two more pirates back, and parried another. The thought sparked in his mind that he had questioned if it was right to wield a blade to kill; but with his own life and those of his friends at stake, he had no choice. Swiftly his fingers remembered their business; he used the pirate's sword as if it were Sodrith.

The Aelenwaith men, Mole saw, held a line near the shore. But the pirates kept coming. "Archers, back!" Mole shouted, hoarse. "Don't shoot at their warriors. Set your arrows afire and shoot for their ships."

Mole fought on, blindly. Later, he did not know how much later, he heard the twang of bows above the shouts of battle. Fire-arrows streaked over the sea to lodge in the rigging of the black ships. Mole's bones ached, but he battled on. His wide strokes toppled pirates to the rocks, and many turned away from him in fear. But his strength was ebbing. More Emnos warriors came at him; and though he thought he might be able to hold two or even three, he could not hold ten.

Then, a crash like thunder came from the bay. On one ship only sails and riggings burned, but the other's hull broke inward like an eggshell in a burst of crimson flame. Blazing shreds of sail fell slowly to the sea, steaming when they met it.

A dozen attackers floundered back to the ship that was still afloat; more splashed toward the flaming smear that had been the other. The men on the rocks shouted. Mole rallied them and led them in a charge that drove the remaining warriors into the breakers. A moment later, the second ship collapsed on the men who were trying to save it. And as the sea with a roar swallowed the burning and dying, the last of the Emnos warriors perished, waist-deep in flaming breakers.

While the men of Aelenwaith gathered around, Mole looked at his stained sword. He plunged it into the sea to clean it, then staggered to shore. Dropping the sword in the sand, he fell to his knees beside it. He was both proud and ashamed of what he had done.

But then, as the mutter of flames died on the sea and strength crept back into his limbs, he began to take long, even breaths. Eyes bright, he pushed himself to his feet, crying out. "Llawer! I understand, Llawer! The sea washed it clean!" Holding the sword in front of him with both hands, he went toward the gathering of Aelenwaith men. As he neared, he shouted the smith's name, looking for him among the townsmen.

Eiddew the Fisherman stopped Mole with a hand on his shoulder. "Don't call for Llawer," he said. "He can't hear you."

The Aelenwaith men moved back to reveal the body of a man, chalk-pale and still, in the sand. Bowing his head, Mole pushed the sword under his belt. Then he helped the other men lift Llawer Smith out of reach of the sea.

· 5 ·

Departures

SQUINTING AT HER target, Merani let an arrow fly. The shaft sang away, glinting slightly before it dived into a bale of straw, into the center, where she had put a shred of red cloth. She felt herself smile as she lowered the bow.

"That was amazing. Can you do that again?"

Merani swallowed her smile. "Do what again?" She looked up, but looked down again, for Prince Ellari, although she hadn't noticed him before, stood next to her on the grass of the castle common.

"That shot you just made," he said, beaming. "I've never seen anything like it. Can you do it again?"

Merani hooked the bow under her arm. "I can try." Fumbling a little, she drew another silver-feathered arrow from her quiver. She wiped her fingers on her sides before she fitted it into the bow.

"Oh, hello, Mair," she heard Ellari say. She glimpsed another shadow join his, but she didn't stop her work to look. "This is something you've got to see. She can hit that bit of cloth on the straw from here. Part of it's that bow of hers; I've never seen a finer one. But she's the best archer in the castle."

Merani, steadying her aim, felt her cheeks flush.

"With all these rumors about goblins," Mair said, "and with both the High King and the High Captain away, it's good to have a warrior or two around. Myself, I wouldn't know which end of the arrow to put against the bowstring."

"That's because you're a lady," Ellari replied. "And that's why we warriors are here—to protect you."

Merani's arrow jerked from her bow; it jolted into the grass a few yards short of her target. She scowled emphatically.

"You were a little off that time, Merani," Ellari said.

"As if I didn't know," Merani muttered. She stormed across the lawn, plucked up her arrow, and snapped it in two. By the time she returned, Ellari seemed to have forgotten all about her; he and Mair spoke to one another in low voices.

"I wouldn't worry if I were you," Ellari said.

"But I can't help worrying," Mair returned, forehead tightening. "It's been four weeks now, Ellari. Four weeks, and he was supposed to be back in two or three!"

Elari shrugged. "Late summer storms slow ships down."

"And sink them."

To this Ellari hooked his thumbs in his belt and frowned. "Mair—"

"You just said yourself there's been no word of him," Mair prodded.

"Not as of this morning. But I'll ask the tower watch again if you want. They may have sighted a ship since noon."

A boy trotted across the lawns. When he reached Merani, he asked, "Lady Merani?" She nodded. She didn't know the boy, but she hoped that Ellari had heard how he had addressed her. "I have message for you. High Princess Geniolien wants to see you. At once."

"Thank you." She moved quickly away, knowing that Ellari and Mair would never miss her.

Merani knew why Geniolien had called her even before she saw the look on the princess's face. Geniolien's hands trembled as she urged Merani inside from the garden. It was as if the sun shone in her eyes, even when they moved into shadow.

"Sit down," Geniolien said, "quickly."

Merani edged into a chair. "You've found it?" she asked.

Geniolien nodded.

"I might be more excited," Merani said, "if I knew what you were looking for. But I'm glad. Did you find it in that stack of scrolls the Chief Minstrel let you look through?"

"No, and I didn't find it in any of those books, either. It wasn't in any of them. What I was looking for was in my head all the time. I should have known, but it didn't strike me until this afternoon. And we've wasted so much time! We have so

little left." Merani wanted to interrupt to ask what they had so
little time for, but Princess Geniolien went on almost without
a breath. "The answer I was looking for comes from a kind of
rhyme I learned as a child, a rhyme I never really understood
until now."

"Let me hear it," Merani said.

After a nod, Geniolien began.

> "In the fastness of the Morning Hills,
> Under Raven Crag, shelled in wood,
> Old Man Oak, older than earth,
> Sends roots into deep magic pools;
> For his red leaves grant all boons."

Somehow disappointed, Merani sat back in her chair. "Is
that all?"

"What more does there need to be?" Geniolien drew her
brows together. "The verse is older than the kings themselves,
and it tells about a person, the Old Man of the Oak, who is
almost as ancient as the mountains themselves and twice as
magical. He works a kind of magic more powerful than almost
any other; it's called earth magic, and it's especially good for
making things strong and for binding things together. The Old
Man of the Oak, or Derwen as he's called in lore books, has
granted wishes for people—some of them my ancestors—for
as long as anybody remembers."

"Then he really exists?"

"Of course," said Geniolien, "and I plan to find him as soon
as I can to ask a wish of him."

"Ask a wish of him?" Merani echoed. "Why?"

Geniolien threw up her hands. "Haven't you listened to
anything I've told you about my dreams and goblin fire and
my brother? Merani, I won't be able to rest until Ranath Drallm
is made safe, once and for all, until there's a spell on the walls
to bind the stones so the goblins won't be able to blast their
way through it. I owe much to my brother, to this castle, and
to all the people who live in it. You've heard all the rumors
about goblins. We may soon have another goblin army camped
between the river and our walls. That's why I've been searching
for books on magic all these days. I want a binding spell for
the walls."

"Why didn't you say so sooner?" Merani sighed. "If you want a spell for the walls, all you have to do is wait until Gwarthan gets back from the war in Crywyll. Have him put one on."

"But I want stronger enchantment than his," Geniolien said. "I want a charm that no necromancer will be able to break. I want earth magic. Only earth magic is strong enough."

"I'm not trying to discourage you," Merani said, "but what makes you think you'll be able to find this Derwen?"

"Finding him shouldn't be hard. Others have done it. Come into my garden, and I'll show you." Merani followed Geniolien from the house onto the steps, where Geniolien pointed toward the mountains in the east. "That verse I told you gives directions enough to find him," Geniolien said. "First of all, he lives in the Morning Hills. That's another name for the Mon Dau."

"But that doesn't help very much. There are lots of mountains in the Mon Dau."

Geniolien smiled. "But only one called Raven Crag. Look, you can see it from here. It's that peak shaped like the top of a raven's head, the one below that tallest mountain. The map-master tells me there's an ancient oak wood in the valley in that mountain's shadow. So when the poem says 'under Raven Crag, shelled in wood,' that's probably what it means. Anyway, it's worth a try, don't you think? Raven Crag's not more than thirty miles over the river from here, so we could make it there and back within a week."

"I'll admit you've got a good head for planning," Merani said, squinting at the mountains, "but don't be hasty. How do you know that this Derwen, if he exists, will want or be able to grant your wish?"

"Tradition," Geniolien answered. "Simply tradition. He's done it before, for at least a dozen people in my family. It was my great-great-grandfather, High King Llarandil, who discovered him in the first place. And almost every High King since has gone to him."

Merani folded her arms. "It sounds too simple to me. If he grants wishes so freely, why isn't everybody in the kingdoms looking for him?"

"He's a secret," Geniolien said. "A family secret."

"It all sounds too easy."

"Easy?" Geniolien said. "Hardly. Going across those miles of goblin-infested wilderness won't be easy. And even finding him will be frightening. He's very powerful and not all good; rather, he's not good or bad. He's not even anywhere between, if you know what I mean."

"Lord Morin will never let you go," Merani said.

"Naturally not. But I'm not going to ask him. I'm not going to tell him, even. In fact, I'm not going to tell anybody I'm going. I am after all the High Princess; the only person with any authority over me is the High King, and he's not here." Geniolien looked determined. "And besides," she added, "I'm as capable of sneaking out of this castle as anybody else!"

"But you yourself said how dangerous it would be. If you're so set on going, you ought at least to take a warrior or two along."

"I am," Geniolien said brightly. She looked at Merani. "You."

Merani's cheeks tingled. She cupped her hands over her mouth. "Me? Is that who you meant when you said 'we'?" She looked again toward Raven Crag. "Why, Geniolien, I'd be happy to go with you, but I think you ought to know I'm not exactly the warrior you think I am—"

"I know that," Geniolien interrupted, "you're a beautiful young lady as well. But you *are* a deadly archer."

Merani thought of her bowshot in front of Ellari. She grimaced. "But Geniolien . . ." She fought for words. "Geniolien, I'm only one person and we might meet dozens of goblins. We ought to take at least one other person along."

"We'll take Cwyller with us, of course. He'll be very helpful in looking for the Old Man of the Oak, once we reach the oak wood."

"Cwyller doesn't count. I mean a warrior, a real warrior."

Geniolien paused. She looked at the trees and fretted with a branch of dying roses. "I'd ask a warrior," she said at length, "but all the ones I know are away in Crywyll."

Merani lifted her eyes. "There's always Prince Ellari."

Supressing a smile, Geniolien asked, "Would he keep our secret?"

"He would if *you* asked him to," Merani said. "He's very obedient; you know how he's been after Prince Berrian to go back to Thrinedor, just because King Ellarwy commanded it. If you, as the High Princess, command him to come with us, he will." Merani adjusted the bow-strap around her shoulder. "Besides," she said, "I think he's rather in awe of your beauty."

"I've heard he's in awe of your skill with the bow, if it comes to that."

Merani's lips formed a hard line. Her eyes fell. But for once Geniolien failed to notice. Instead, the princess smiled absently.

"We will leave tonight," she said.

When morning came, everything was grey: the sea, the sky, the spray, the rocks, and even the mountain in its quilt of mist. The townspeople of Eber Ynys lined the beach, shivering as the wind rippled their cloaks. King Eiddew stood a little apart from them, near a small vessel that rose and fell on the swells. The boat, the first from Eiddew the Fisherman's shops near the cliff, groaned a little in the shifting water, and the wind played with the knots that held its sail furled.

"I ask you again to stay," King Eiddew said to Mole. "The autumn storms are beginning, and the winter storms will follow. Stay with us until spring, here in Ynys, where you may keep a little drier."

"Wet or dry, I've got to go," Mole answered. "I don't like the look of the weather, either, but if I don't return to Drallm soon . . ." His voice lost itself in the crash of the waves, for he could not remember how many weeks had passed since he left Ranath Drallm. "If I waited until spring," Mole resumed, "they would all think I was dead."

"I won't hold you, then," King Eiddew said, "though I'll be afraid for you."

"When you first came," Eiddew the Fisherman broke in, "I would have thrown stones at you to keep you away. Now I would throw stones at you if I thought it could keep you here."

"Yes," said a woman from the crowd. "When you are gone, who will cheer us this winter, now that we have lost Llawer Smith?"

Mole flinched. "You will all have to cheer each other," he said. "And if I stayed, I don't think I'd be much cheer to you. But I will miss you—all of you. Part of me will always be in Aelenwaith. But I must go. The *Taran-y-Mor* is so long overdue that I know it has perished. And I'm afraid the same evil that claimed the *Taran-y-Mor* may be claiming far more. I've seen Serenwawn burning in the north, like a beacon calling me home."

"The storm that sank the *Taran-y-Mor* may swallow you," someone protested.

"And you've practiced sailing only two days," another added.

"At least let one of us come with you."

Mole stepped into the boat. "No." He laid the ash staff in the bottom of the boat, weighted it down with a water cask, then held his hand up toward the people of the town. "I'm ready now."

"Loose the moorings," King Eiddew commanded.

While Eiddew the Fisherman cut the cords that anchored the bow of the vessel to the beach, some of Good Eiddew's Men tugged it from the rocks. As the boat rode the first wave, Mole set his sail, the wind filled the canvas, and the boat slid over the first breaker, thudded into a second, and broke the third with an explosion of spray.

King Eiddew stood thigh-deep in the sea. "You'll always have a friend in the King of Aelenwaith!" he cried. "Do I have the same promise from you?"

"Yes!" Mole shouted back. "Yes! Farewell!"

The king turned back toward the beach, where the townspeople waved and called across the water to Mole.

"Good-bye!" Mole shouted.

The seawall soon vanished behind the promontory of rocks; the houses of Eber Ynys melted into the greyness. Wind drove the boat at such speed that Mole found strength only to hold the tiller against the waves. And soon he turned the boat from the fading island toward the emptiness northward.

Fflad, Mole knew, would insist on naming the vessel. But Fflad was poetic and clever, and the only names Mole could think of sounded dull or overdone. He felt the spray on his cheeks, watching the northward surge of the waves for a long time before finally, patting the stern, he whispered, *"Arien."*

Arien. Mole smiled at the thought, for he could hear her voice even now. "By the Emperor, Mole, if you'd taken any longer to get back from Aelenwaith, I'd have turned to stone. All I can say is that I hope you found that treasure you were looking for! If I weren't so glad to see you, I wouldn't give you the tunic I've been embroidering for you all summer!" Mole laughed to himself. He began to hear other things Arien might say to him, and he spent that morning thinking about Fflad and Arien and how much they looked like one another, now that he thought about it. He anticipated the look on Arien's face when he told her Fflad was her brother.

He found dried meat and biscuits to eat at noon; but he never finished his meal, for a storm came up.

Screaming against the sail, the wind drove darts of rain across the face of the ocean, which moaned at the onset of the storm. At first Mole thought the storm was only a passing squall, but the wind rose, closing the clouds overhead. Swells crested into hills, then into mountains. Wild blasts of wind nearly pitched the boat on its side. Rain drenched Mole as he tried to take down the sail.

But already it was too late. For now the waves shivered in a wind whose icy edge, Mole realized, could only have been made by sorcery. It froze the ropes under a layer of ice, welding them together, making the sail rigid against the wind.

The storm hurled the vessel westward along a wavecrest. Falling to the bottom of the boat, Mole met salt water. He dragged himself up, gripping the mast to gain his feet, but a wave poured over the gunwale and doused him. As the boat lurched forward again, he hugged the mast, pressing his cheek to the wood as the next wave came.

Some time later thunder pealed overhead. "The sail!" Mole said between gritted teeth. "The sail's got to come down, or I'll drown!" Gulping for air, he shoved himself away from the mast. But as he lifted the canvas into his arms, a wave beat him against the side of the boat, and he sank into senselessness.

The next thing he knew, the vessel was spinning crazily. It seemed to be sliding backward, downhill. Mole soon saw that aft of the boat a valley gaped, wider than any carved by a river. "Emperor save me!" he gasped.

Then the ship lurched. Mole's head struck the mast. He remembered no more of the storm.

In the coldest hour before dawn, Arien awoke. It was completely dark in her room; she could see no more than a brushing of grey in the blackness where her fire might be. She trembled from the cold. Even when she tightened her blanket around her, she shivered.

At last, when she could find no remedy for the cold, she got up, wincing when her feet met the floor. She ran to her hearth, then kneeling beside it, held her palm over it, but felt only faint heat. She fumbled for more tinder, then for more wood, but she could find neither. So she laid her fingers in the ashes, pressed her eyes closed, and concentrated fiercely.

Flames sprang up around her hand. She drew her arm quickly back as the fire licked across the heap of ashes to consume the black remnants of logs. Arien sighed as the warmth closed over her, but her extended hands suddenly curled when she realized what she had done. She bit her fist in frustration.

"If you use it," she reminded herself, "it will only grow faster."

The thought frightened her. She could feel a spark in the back of her mind, a spark that had been born weeks before. Closing her eyes, she could see that it had grown now; it was a speck of light no longer. It was more a smear, a dish-shaped glow on the curtain of her consciousness. Quickly she opened her eyes again.

She returned to bed, but not to sleep. Instead, she brought from under her mattress a length of black cloth. In the firelight she saw the stretch of embroidery she had done the week after Mole left for Aelenwaith; it was a leafy design in blues and greens like falling water. Beyond it the thread formed gold flowers among the leaves; but the leaves themselves turned gold as well, then orange, then red. They became thinner, more angled, brighter until they looked like flames. Yet they were not flames, no more than the blaze Arien had brought to the hearth was fire.

Without knowing why she did so, Arien snatched up a needle and groped for thread, beginning to stitch where the cloth was empty. She scarcely saw the pattern she formed, only the glitter of her moving needle. She sewed faster, sewed in a frenzy of long stitches, for she realized suddenly that her fingers were painting an answer her mind only half knew, the answer to a riddle she had not dared ask over the long weeks since her power had begun to grow. Twice in her frenzy she pricked herself, but if blood came, she did not see it. She saw only her pattern taking shape.

Then it was finished, and she gazed at it in wonder.

Though she had used only gold thread, the design flamed with a dozen colors, reds and oranges, whites and greys. The bottom of her work formed a black horizon, the top a ring of dark cloud; in between, painfully exquisite, was the fire of sunrise on the face of the sky.

"Dawn," she whispered, cold again. "Dawn." She put the cloth aside and reached under her pillow, brought out the white book, whose cover, gold in the fireglow, was still warm where her hand had rested on it through the night. She opened it hastily and ran her finger down the familiar lines of a poem. Her finger stopped, and she murmured:

> "And when wars and warlocks all are gone
> Will Amreth's daughters seek the dawn."

Her fingers, suddenly, were so numb with cold that she dropped the book. Looking to the hearth, she at first saw flames, but realized that they were only illusion, the sparkle on the crystalline ashes of the first shaft of pale dawn light through her window. Looking at dawn's faint glow on the glass, she folded her hands together and drew up her legs under her. She closed her eyes to block out the light, but the spark inside her mind showed her even a broader panorama of dawn light, glittering like fire.

A knock on her door awakened her. She hurried to open it.

It was Prince Berrian. His face was drawn, his cheeks empty. He looked as if he had dressed hurriedly, for his jacket was only half buttoned, and his hair was tangled. "Arien!" he said, before she could speak, "Arien, come quickly. It's Fflad. He's not well. Not well at all."

"Not well? That can't be! I saw him only yesterday, and he seemed to be doing better. He talked to me for hours, and we ate together at noon. He's been getting better all these weeks—"

"He's taken a sudden turn for the worse. Arien, you must come *now*. The healing masters say he is near death—"

Arien seized her cloak and flung it around her shoulders. "Let's run," she said to Berrian.

Together they hurried across the lawns toward the Bards' Quarter. A watery light came into the sky from the east, casting damp shadows behind the trees. Though Arien could not match his strides, Berrian gave her his arm to help her keep up with him. She nearly fell once on the long flight of dim stairs, but Berrian caught her and half carried her up the last few steps to Fflad's door.

They found Fflad in the light of three waning candles. He lay perfectly still with closed eyes. His skin, waxlike, seemed so transparent that Arien fancied she could see his skull under his cheeks, the bones in his arms. She touched his forehead to find it like fire, but like a fire that had turned to coals, for it cast no light over his sunken features.

"He has a fever," she told the two healing masters who stood on the opposite side of the bed. "Bring cloths and water, quickly."

One of the healing masters laid a hand on a pail at the side of the bed, and the other held up a cloth. "We've used all our art to help him. We have bathed his forehead since midnight and administered our most powerful herbs. But it does no good."

"You certainly can do something," Arien said.

"We have already done much," said the other healing master.

"One or the other of you must know what's wrong with him," Berrian broke in. "My father's healers in Thrinedor, they couldn't always cure a sickness, but at least they always knew what it was."

"Oh, we know what it is. That's why we sent for you. For we have watched this same sickness before, and we know that your friend won't live to see morning."

Berrian and Arien looked at one another. Arien wondered if her own face was the color of Berrian's. "Are you sure?" Berrian asked.

Neither of the healers replied, but both nodded.

Arien's hand suddenly stiffened. "Berrian," she said, "I need to be with Fflad alone. Just for a moment."

"But do you think you ought to be? No, I'll stay with you, Arien."

Arien pointed at the healers. "You," she said, almost sharply, "as long as there isn't anything you can do for him, let us be alone." As the healers left, she turned to Berrian. "I would appreciate it if you went with them, too. Give me a few minutes alone with Fflad. Please. He's almost like my brother. I've got to be alone with him!"

"I understand," Berrian said, "but I won't let you be long."

As soon as Berrian had gone, Arien pressed the door closed, bolting it behind her. Swiftly she blew out the candles, sat on the edge of Fflad's bed, then concentrated on Fflad's face until she could make it out in the soft dawn light. She reached for Fflad's hand, but hesitated; when she closed her eyes, she saw flames now, flames she could feel trembling in her veins even before she called the power from her mind. She bit her tongue.

"Arien," she told herself, lifting her hands away, "you've got to be careful; you can't use very much, not so soon." She glanced at the traces of light in the trees beyond Fflad's window. "If you use enough to save him," she heard herself say, "the power may bring your time this very day. You may lose yourself to the world, to Mole."

She began to cry. Quiet, burning tears glistened on her cheeks. "Arien," she said at last, "Arien, don't be a selfish fool." She looked at Fflad again, and seeing the familiar curl of his lips, the pleasant curve of his fingers, she reached down and snatched up his hand. She smoothed it against her palm, then held it fast as she squeezed her eyes closed.

She saw sparks like trails of fire or falling stars. She felt her own hand grow warm while Fflad's grew cool. "Powers of Amreth," she muttered, "burn away his sickness, fill him with the fire of life." Her hands trembled. Fire roared in her ears. She felt her will draining away to be replaced by an empty loneliness, the kind of coldness she had felt that morning, a coldness that longed to be warmed by the blaze of fire in her mind. For a moment she hung between the fire and the darkness, unwilling to choose either, but with a final effort, she dropped Fflad's hand, threw her own hands to her face, and tried to close the darkness around the ring of fire in her mind. Yet it blazed now so brightly that she could see it even with her eyes open, and the harder she tried to quench it, the more furiously it burned. Panting, she reeled up from the bed. She screamed. Not because the fire was unpleasant, but because she could not contain it.

Then, slowly at first, she began to push it back. She molded it into a spherical glow, then back into a single point of fire. Breathing hard, she forced the spark under a veil of blackness. She could feel the awakened power straining against its brittle bond, and she knew that if she called on the fire again, used even the dimmest spark of enchantment, the binding would shatter, and the fire would grow beyond her control, until it became what she had sewn on the cloth, the Great Fire of dawn.

"I will never touch the power again," she murmured, gritting her teeth at the stripes of dawn beyond the river, "never, never, never, no matter how much I want to use it. I won't let it claim me!" She thought of Mole, touched his memory, and made a silent promise to him. "Never," she said. Yet the power shifted in her like a chained wolf, threatening to break free even as she thought of it.

A few birds piped beyond the glittering square of Fflad's window. Arien looked at Fflad. His chest rose and fell with easy breaths, his face held a soft, healthful color. Smiling, Arien took his hand again. It was cool and firm.

Startled, she heard Berrian's voice at the door. "Arien? Are you all right? Let me in!"

Moving to the door, she slid back the bolt. "Arien," Berrian said, seizing her arm. "I was at the bottom of the stairs when I heard you scream. Is Fflad . . . is Fflad . . . dead?"

"Dead? Oh, no. I just screamed when I saw . . . how quickly he recovered."

Berrian's eyebrows fell. "Recovered?"

"Look for yourself," Arien said. She moved aside. Berrian brushed past her to kneel at Fflad's bedside. He examined Fflad for several minutes before turning to Arien in puzzled joy.

"Arien! He looks better than he has for weeks! What happened?"

Arien shrugged. "Sometimes the healers don't know as much as they think they do. Perhaps Fflad was only suffering from a bit of fever. He was fine yesterday, and I think he'll be fine today, though we ought to keep visiting him until he recovers completely."

"But he was near death! I know he was." Berrian stared at her. "Arien, there's something you're not telling me. Did you heal him?"

"I did nothing to heal him," Arien said. "I only guided the force that did." She said no more, but Berrian seemed to understand.

"Fellheath!" he said, a sudden light on his face. "Fellheath! You did the same thing on Fellheath. You healed Mole, though you pretended you didn't, when the rest of us thought he was dead."

She turned her face away. "It was easier then."

"Arien! Do you realize the gift you have, the power? You could become the greatest healing master in the kingdoms. Think of all those who are sick and near death in this castle. Think of all those who will be wounded when the High King returns from the west—"

"Berrian!" she said. "Berrian, no!"

He blinked at her.

"Don't tell anyone about my power or about what you have seen here," she said in a quieter voice. "For I will never, I must never, *never* use it again."

• 6 •

Where Good Men Rest

"BLAST!" MOLE SAID. He rubbed his swollen eyes, then probed at the bumps on his head. Something whined in his ears, and there was a salty taste in his mouth. Sitting up, he spat emphatically while he waited for his blotched vision to clear.

Odors of salt and sea stung his nostrils. Waves lapped the warm planks where he lay. His back felt sticky. Looking around, he saw the blue of sea and sky under the hot noon sun. His boat, what was left of it, lay heavy on the sea; water pooled around his legs, and each wave that struck the ship sent water through a long crack in the planks of the bulwarks. The sail had vanished, all but a few fluttering rags, and the yardarm was gone as well, and with it the top half of the mast.

Mole blinked at the destruction. He tried to swallow, but his throat hurt too much. He soon saw that the ash staff, caught between two timbers, had not been lost. He picked it up and propped it against his shoulder.

"I ought to be happy I'm alive," he croaked to himself, "but that's not much comfort if I'm going to starve to death out here." He realized that without a sail and without provisions, he had little chance of reaching land alive.

The sun passed behind a cloud, and when the glare lifted from the water, Mole saw running along one horizon what he wanted to see most.

Land.

He wondered whether the storm had blown him all the way home.

But the landforms didn't look familiar. To the right, gentle hills rose, thick with trees on the very edge of the beach. He saw on the left a sweep of grey-purple, probably heathland, that fell away to a stretch of blue, a bay or perhaps a river mouth. The brownish tint in the water seemed to indicate a river, and in the center of it, a black island rose like a huge ship.

Mole found himself drawn to the island. Not only was it odd in shape, very steep and pointed, but it also seemed to be all of black rock. On the brink of the island, notches stood out in the green haze of the river; they seemed to be fortifications of some kind. The island cast a long, baleful shadow over the sea, a shadow that seemed to reach toward Mole.

Then Mole realized where he was; the sea had temporarily confused him. The hilly country on the east was the Great Forest of Pesten; the land on the west, the southern mead-country of Crywyll. The river could be only the Widewater or Ystadun. And the island, the island was the tutory of sorcerers, Dragonshead.

Mole shuddered. He remembered the High King's plan to bring war to the river mouth, to defeat Branddabon. But whether the king had lost or won, the coasts of Pesten and Crywyll did not tell. The battle was over now, and Dragonshead brooded in silence.

"The gale blew me farther than I ever imagined," Mole said. "Now I'm farther from Drallm than I was in Aelenwaith, and I don't have any provisions." He wanted to say more, but the shadow of Dragonshead seemed to shift, headlike, toward him.

Yet the shore, too, seemed nearer than it had when Mole had first seen it. The boat, apparently, was drifting toward the Pesten shore, not, happily, toward the island in the river mouth. But the hull was beginning to leak freely, and the aft of the ship could soon sink into the water, so Mole began baling with his hands, for lack of anything better. But because his effort seemed to do little good, he took up a plank and began paddling with it.

The gap between boat and shore closed slowly, and Mole's rowing seemed only to spin the vessel. Within an hour, the aft of the boat vanished under water; Mole climbed to the bow, which tilted upward as the beach neared. Finally, at some distance from the shore, the back of the boat scraped a rock. The boat became still, and its prow began to sink beneath him. So, using the staff as a float, he leaped from the boat and swam toward shore.

When he dragged himself onto the beach, he could see only the tip of the boat above the breakers. He lay in the sand for a long time, for in spite of the evening shadows, it was still warm from the day's sun. And when at last he sat up, he spent a few minutes brushing wet sand from his clothes and out of his hair.

Night neared. Stripes of shadow washed over the sea, and shadows lengthened across the beach from the forest. The nip of wind and the rust color of the leaves spoke of autumn, and though the days would be mild this far south, the nights would be cold. Especially without blankets or fire or food. And there were no settlements nearby. The rising hills along the beach were a wild wood, where food would be hard to find, where Mole might meet more enemies than friends. And in the west, Dragonshead was shrouded in gloom.

"I'll have a long walk back to Drallm," Mole said, "and I won't have a sword to fight any goblins I meet on the way." But he knew that he had no choice but to walk if he wanted to see Arien again.

He started eastward at once along the beach, knowing it would be safest to keep away from the trees. He judged it best to go until his strength failed, because every mile he put between himself and Dragonshead would make him more secure. The evil it radiated was actually visible, twisting the roots and distorting the leaves of the trees.

Then suddenly he stopped. For a moment he didn't know why. But soon he saw footprints in the sand below him, above where the waves came. They were faint and certainly several weeks old, but there were many of them, of different and confused kinds. Among them was a smooth place in the sand, as if something had been dragged along in the middle of their company. The tracks disappeared in the dead grass at the edge of the beach.

Something told Mole to go on, but something also told him to follow the tracks, something deep inside him that seemed to sense something wrong. Something evil, certainly, but something more, something tragic, waiting for him beyond the trees.

He hesitated. But he turned from the sea to follow the footprints from the beach. Though he was no tracker, he could see the path the makers of the prints had used, a gravelly ravine under trees that ended at a small hill crowned with a ring of alders.

The grove wasn't as easy to reach as Mole had expected. Briars choked the ravine, and crooked trees barred his way; loose gravel blanketed with damp leaves made uneasy footing. But something drew Mole, something that made him ignore all the difficulties.

He soon climbed to the hilltop. Pushing past the first tree trunks, he found himself in what seemed to be almost a room. The branching alders overhead made a roof that no light pierced; their trunks seemed to be columns or perhaps bars. The darkness below the leaves was both musty and oppressive, and Mole kept thinking insects were dropping on him from the branches above.

He felt gloom and decided to leave at once.

But something made him stay. He could just make out an oblong of earth free of leaves in the center of the alder ring. The earth of the oblong seemed to have been recently upturned and loosely replaced, as if the diggers had been in a hurry. Stranger still, from the loose clods a few tiny flowers had sprung up, pale in the twilight under the trees.

Flowers in autumn, and in the shade of trees? They could be here, Mole realized, for only one reason. *Blossoms bloom where good men rest.* One of the poets had said something like that. But so many flowers; Mole could see dozens of them now, strewn like fallen stars over the loose earth.

This was a grave, the grave of a great man, a bard or a warrior perhaps, but most likely a king. Sensing sadness and solemnity, but horror and unhappiness as well, Mole tried to recall any king or hero who had died in these lands. But he could think of no one. And the grave had been filled only recently—

He clenched the ash staff with the sudden thought, *Gion*.

Mole bowed his head, for the thought seemed to strike truth. The battle against Branddabon must have gone amiss. Fierce with sorrow, Mole bent to touch the earth of the grave.

But another thought made him bring his head up. The grave couldn't be Gion's. It couldn't be. The High King, Mole knew, was wise enough not to underestimate the enemy's power; the relative peace of the landscape seemed to indicate his victory.

Also, even if the king had been slain, no one would have laid him to rest in the deep forest. He would have been taken back to Drallm and there laid in a tomb with his ancestors. Mole stood up and turned to go. Someone great had been buried here, but not the High King. Living or dead, the High King would be at Drallm.

Ranath Drallm! If only it were nearer. If only he were there now. In the failing light, the world seemed to close on him like a trap; Mole came from the brambles to the beach in time to see Orygath, the brighter of the pole stars, prick out above the trees. Yet other stars were coming out, most of them faint and veiled. And in the east, between the sea and the rising full moon, a bright star burned red, like a torch in the sky.

• 7 •

The Goblin Lair

DUSK GATHERED IN the valley below them. The final rays of the sun swept across the highlands, lighting the oaks on the ridge in red. A mist poured out of the canyons to erase the glimmer of stars over the looming eastern mountains. The shell of the moon hovered over Raven Crag. Below it, an uncommonly bright star burned near the face of the peak, as if it were a beacon set on the mountain.

They climbed the rocky slopes of the mountain, moving up out of a wooded valley where a noisy stream ran. The wood toward which they struggled seemed even less cheerful than the one they had just left; a few tattered leaves clung to their branches, but most of their boughs were bare, not only of leaves but also of bark. The trees looked like bones in the odd light, and the boulders among them like eyeless skulls half-buried in the mountain.

Halfway up from the valley to the ridge, Merani stopped to adjust her pack and to look back over the lowlands. "I don't see Cwyller," she said. "He must have found something interesting or he'd be back by now."

"Probably he found searchers back in woodland," Geniolien said. "The whole castle's probably looking for us now, because in my note I said we'd be gone two weeks at the most."

Ellari hooked his thumbs in the straps of his backpack. "I don't know how I let you talk me into coming with you," he said, shaking his head. "If I'd known we'd be gone *three weeks* and still be nowhere near our destination, nothing you said could have talked me into coming with you."

Geniolien sighed. "Sometimes it's better when we don't know what's in store for us."

Ellari smiled blandly. "We should have brought horses," he said.

"Yes, we should have," Merani said.

"If we'd brought horses, we wouldn't have gotten this far," Geniolien returned. "We couldn't possibly have taken horses through the secret passage, and if we'd ridden through the gate, the guards would have stopped us."

"*I* should have stopped you," Ellari said. He sat down on a rock and put his chin in his hands. "I should never have let you go. This is dangerous. It's been dangerous for three weeks. *I* should have been responsible and saved us all this walking."

"Raven Crag *is* farther from Drallm than it looks," Geniolien admitted.

"That's not what I mean. I mean it's ironic that I, my father's most trustworthy son, should go off on an adventure when I'm supposed to be bringing Berrian back to Thrinedor."

"I'm sure Berrian will put in a good word for you," Merani said.

"Well, it won't do us any good too look back," Geniolien said. "As long as we've come this far, we'd better finish what we came here to do. Raven Crag can't be more than a day or two away."

"That's what you said last week," Ellari said, glaring at her.

"Then one of these weeks," Geniolien said brightly, "I'm bound to be right. And we ought at least to make it up this hill before we bed down for the night. If there's enough dry wood up there, we can make ourselves a fire and have a cheerful firelight supper."

"Supper? With what? We're running low on food, you know. Especially considering that it has to last till we get back to Drallm."

"I told Cwyller to watch for food as well as enemies," Merani said. "Maybe that's why he's taking so long. He might have found some."

"The only food walking around in these mountains is us," Ellari said. He touched his sword. "At least from the goblin point of view. We are in goblin country. I don't think that lighting a fire tonight would be a good idea."

Merani thought she saw faint lights on the hills, lights that were most likely cookfires for goblins and outlaws. She preferred to think of neither, for with Cwyller's help, they managed to avoid both groups so far.

Cwyller returned when they had almost reached the trees. He swooped suddenly to Merani's shoulder before anyone had noticed him, so none of them could tell from what direction he had come.

"Well," Ellari said, after Cwyller had bobbed on Merani's arm for several moments, keening, "has he found anything to eat?"

"I don't know, but he's found something, something that excited him a lot, though I don't understand what it is. *He* doesn't quite understand what it is. It seems to be at the top of this hill, whatever it is. He wants us to follow him."

"Follow him to what?" Ellari asked. "A goblin camp?"

"Cwyller's smarter than that," Merani retorted. "He wouldn't lead us to something if it wasn't safe."

"But how does he know what's safe? He's only a bird."

"Only a bird?" Merani burst out. "Only a bird? If he's only a bird, you're only a common boy! He's a white hawk, a hawk of the royal breed of Vivrandon. You ought to know that much—" Merani interrupted herself by clapping her hand over her mouth, for she realized she was shouting. Ellari, folding his arms, turned away from her. "Ellari," she began in a thin voice, "I didn't mean to—"

"Merani," Geniolien broke in, "your hawk is halfway to the forest. Let's follow him. He hasn't led us into danger before. Come on."

By the time they reached the first trees, it was dark. Merani could see Cwyller only as a white shadow in the black branches of a barren pine. When they approached, he flew from his perch to another tree just on the edge of sight; he repeated this every time they neared him, leading them deeper into the pinewood. The ground was stony, so all of them had trouble keeping their footing in the dark. Merani noticed larger formations of rock behind the trees, rock walls, upcroppings of boulders, and piles of stones. It was almost as if they were among ruins.

At length, when the stars were ablaze overhead, Cwyller stopped. He poised on the bough of a hemlock tree and began cawing, crowlike. They halted.

"This must be it," Geniolien said. She looked around her.

"But what is it? I don't see anything but rocks and trees."

"I do," Ellari said, freezing. He pointed past the hemlock tree. "There."

Merani looked. Set in a rock face was a door. Rather there were two doors, both made of heavy, rough wood bound with iron. One lay closed, but the other stood open, revealing a rectangle of blackness behind it. All of them stared at it except Ellari, who drew his sword and approached the door to sniff at the darkness.

"What is it?" Geniolien whispered.

Ellari made a face. "Goblins," he said. "By the stench, I'd say a lot of them, a short time ago. Or maybe still," he added with a glance at the door.

"Then this is a goblin lair," Geniolien said.

Ellari nodded. "And a strange one. I've gone goblin hunting with my father in Thrinedor. I've seen dozens of lairs; they're almost always in rocky places, in caves, in pits, in gullies. But I've never seen one with doors before. Goblins usually don't build."

"Then this must have been built by someone else," Merani reasoned. "It must have been something else before it was a goblin lair."

"Yes. But what?" Stooping, Ellari peered into the darkness. "It doesn't look like a place men would live in; and besides, we're too high up in the mountains to be near any settlements."

"Then it must be a trove of some kind."

Merani and Ellari looked at one another, but Geniolien stepped between them. "Whatever it used to be," she said, "it's a goblin lair now, and we'd better leave before they come back—or come out!"

"If there were any goblins near," Ellari said, "we'd hear them. They're noisy brutes; they're positively incapable of being quiet. The ones that live here must be out hunting. We're quite safe for the time being. Let's have a look inside."

"I thought you were the one who wanted to avoid danger," Merani said.

"But this isn't dangerous. I've been goblin hunting before, and when you come to a goblin lair that's empty, it usually stays empty until the goblins come back just before dawn. And most goblin lairs have treasure in them, gold and jewels that the goblins have plundered."

"But what if they left a guard behind?" Geniolien protested.

"Oh, Ellari! We brought you along because we thought you were sensible. Let's go."

"Give me a minute to look around first. It won't take long."

"If you're going in," Merani said, "I'm going with you."

"If both of you go in," Geniolien said, "I don't want to have to stall goblins at the door for you. I'm going along." But she glared at Ellari.

Bending down, Ellari disappeared into the darkness. Merani took a deep breath and followed him. She plunged into a darkness that smelled like a kennel that had not been cleaned for some time. The odor grew worse as she half-walked, half-crawled down a kind of low tunnel. She kept imagining eyes glowing ahead and clawed hands reaching out from the walls.

When Geniolien screamed, Merani's head met the roof.

"Geniolien!" she heard Ellari call. "Princess Geniolien? Are you all right?"

"Spiderwebs!" Geniolien's voice returned, sounding distant. "Spiderwebs!"

"Is that all," Merani shouted back. "You almost scared me to death! Next time you scream for help, make sure you need it first."

"I didn't scream for help. I just screamed."

"How are we supposed to know the difference?"

"I think we're out of the tunnel, now," Ellari said. His voice echoed slightly. "This lair seems to be pretty big."

Merani straightened. She reached upward but could feel nothing.

"There," said Geniolien. "Now we've seen the lair. Now let's go back."

Ellari didn't answer her. Merani heard him shuffling about, picking things up. Something clanked.

"Treasure?" Merani asked.

"A cook pot," Ellari said. "Not very clean, either."

"Personally," Geniolien broke in, "I don't like the idea of feeling around in the darkness. You never know what you might find. If it's treasure you want, Ellari, I've got plenty of it back at Ranath Drallm, and I'll give you all you want when we get home."

Ellari didn't seem to hear her. "I've found a water flask," he said in a moment. "What a piece of luck. We didn't think to bring one."

"*I'm* not drinking from it," Geniolien said.

"The goblins haven't been using it, if that's what you mean. It's not one of *theirs*. They must have stolen it from somebody, because it's made out of doeskin and . . . silver, I think. It's well crafted."

"Good," Geniolien said. "You've found your treasure. Now let's go."

"Not for just a minute," Ellari said.

Meanwhile Merani squatted where she stood. She touched the floor. It was cold, hard, and somewhat damp. She probed around her feet with her hand. Something brushed against her finger, tinkling. She picked it up. It seemed to be a ring, a plain ring by the feel of it. She meant to announce her discovery, but Ellari was talking about some shields he had found, so she said nothing, and for lack of a pocket, slipped it on her finger. She'd been certain it would be too big, but it seemed to fit perfectly. Reaching out farther, she touched something hard and smooth. Though it seemed to be rock, it was too round and polished to be a stone. Her fingers probed it curiously until her thumb sank into an eye-sized hole.

"Oooh!" she said, standing up and drawing her hand away. "How awful!"

"What is it?" Geniolien and Ellari said, almost at the same time.

"A skull," Merani said, "a skull! Let's get out of here. Now!"

"That's not so bad," Ellari soothed. "You always find that kind of thing in goblin lairs. Grim, but not unusual. If you want to leave now, though, we will. Just let me find you again, and we'll go up the passage together." Merani heard Ellari making his way across the stones. Suddenly he said, "Sorry about your foot, Geniolien."

"What about my foot?"

"I stepped on it, didn't I? I said I was sorry."

"It's not *my* foot," Geniolien said in a shaky voice.

"It's not mine, either," Merani said. "Ellari—"

She heard Ellari shout and rip his sword from his sheath. Sparks flashed, and something crashed on the stones.

"Ellari!" Merani shouted, backing toward the tunnel mouth. "Ellari!"

He chuckled, then burst out laughing.

"Ellari!" Geniolien shouted. "What's wrong?"

"I've just killed my first log," Ellari replied. "I must have stepped on its root and thought it was your foot. Then its branch touched me. I thought it was a goblin. I thought I was dead—"

"You're lucky not to be," Geniolien said, "of fright if nothing else. Now, let's leave this place at once!"

They found Cwyller on the same hemlock branch, preening himself. When Merani emerged from the lair, he flashed away into the sky.

"He'll find out if any goblins are near," Merani said.

"Whether there are or not, we shouldn't stay here," Ellari said. "We'd better put a good distance between us and this lair before we sleep. The goblins are likely to come after us when they see that their lair's been disturbed. Maybe we'd better wade in a few streams, too, so they won't be able to follow our scent."

"All this," Geniolien said, "for a water flask!"

And a ring, Merani thought. But she said nothing.

They walked in moonlight for several hours without seeing any sign of goblins. Cwyller returned and poised himself calmly on Merani's shoulder. How many valleys, ridges, and copses they crossed, Merani could not afterward remember; she knew only that they had splashed across the same streams over and over again, climbed a steep canyon wall, and watched the moon sink behind the hills before they at last slept.

The sun was already high when Merani awoke. Its light slanted down through the gold leaves of aspen trees, among which they had camped. As she rubbed the sleep from her eyes and the grass from her hair, she heard the roar of a mountain river not far off.

At first she could see neither Ellari nor Geniolien, but when she stood up, she saw Ellari some distance away, sharpening his sword on a rock. He waved to her and shouted her name. Merani smiled back, because Ellari rarely said good morning to her. Perhaps, she thought, his goblin treasure had put him in a good mood. She did not see Geniolien, but she knew where the princess had gone.

She found Geniolien at the edge of the stream, combing her hair. She had unbound it and it fell like black water from her head, its ends not far from the stream. The princess was humming something, but when Merani came near, she stopped her song and smiled.

"Good morning. We thought we'd let you sleep, since you seemed to be able to, and since we were walking almost till dawn."

Merani knelt on the streambank. "Any goblins?"

"Would you have slept so late if there were?" Geniolien laughed. "Your hawk went away as soon as dawn came, but he didn't seem to find anything—nothing but a sparrow for breakfast, that is."

Merani dipped her hands in the stream, but she held them suddenly still, for something glittered on her finger. It was a moment before she remembered about the ring and could finish splashing water across her hands. And when she had dried them on her cape, she looked at the ring again. It seemed to be only a plain band of silver, yet it glittered like diamond-speckled gold. And something about the way the sun sparkled on it made her hands look beautiful as well, as if they were no longer red and calloused, but white and smooth instead.

"It's probably the water," Merani muttered.

"What was that?"

"This water's awfully cold," Merani said. "Tell me, Geniolien. Do you think I could go without a wash this morning?"

Throwing back her hair, Geniolien studied her. "If you want to know the truth, you could get by. In fact," Geniolien went on, turning her head sideways, "it looks as if you've washed already." A pause followed, during which Geniolien seemed increasingly puzzled. "Merani," she said in a low voice, "Ellari was right."

"What was Ellari right about?"

"You." Geniolien smiled. "I thought he was crazy when he said it, but I see now why he did."

Merani reddened under Geniolien's stare. "What did he say?"

"You were still asleep," Geniolien said, "but Ellari and I were awake, talking. We were discussing goblins, but he kept looking away, at you. Then out of nowhere he said, 'You know something, Geniolien. I've just realized she's a girl.' 'Of course she is,' I said, but I didn't take time to look at you because I wanted to come and wash. 'I mean, I've *known* she was a girl all along,' he said, 'but I just *realized* it a moment ago.' I finally know what he meant. You look different somehow, Merani."

"What does that mean?" Merani said.

"It means you're *especially* pretty today. You just seem to— glow. It's not your clothes, and it's not your hair, although the sun does make it look more gold than red. And it's not your eyes. It's something in your face, Merani. You look like yourself, but you don't. I can't explain it."

Merani wanted to say that she couldn't explain it, either, but then she remembered the ring. She thrust the hand with the ring on it behind her back, struck by the truth of what had happened. "I've always heard that mountain air does wonders for you," she said at last. "It must be especially good for me."

"Apparently," Geniolien said.

Merani excused herself and started up the hill, hiding the ring in her hand. At first she felt bad about deceiving Geniolien and keeping the ring a secret. But, after all, it wasn't every day that she found an enchanted ring. And, she reasoned, didn't she deserve the chance to be beautiful without anybody questioning how she had become that way?

But the best reason of all, she knew, waited for her in the aspens, sharpening his sword on the rocks.

Mole saw it first through a screen of autumn leaves. It was almost as if he had suddenly come on a gem in a sunlit clearing, for it was there without warning, beyond the fringes of the wood, sparkling like a crystal in a circle of sunlight. He stopped, stared at the fortress on the hill, unwilling to believe, almost, that he had reached it. Then he shouted at the top of his voice, threw the staff into the air, caught it, and burst out from the last trees.

So many nights he had dreamed of those walls gleaming in the moonlight, and so many days he had longed to see them rise above the trees. But the somber autumn forest had been endless, broken only by leaf-covered ruins and wide stretches of beach. It had been a lean walk, too; Mole had eaten little more than berries and a few fish. He also carried a red semicircle on one hand, the badge of his wrestling match with a goblin that had come on him in the night.

"Thank the Emperor," he repeated over and over again as he climbed the castle hill. "Thank the Emperor I'm home." He tried to absorb all the details of his homecoming, the familiar smells in the air, the familiar look of the walls, but he was so weary that he could barely plod his way to the gate.

"Arien," he muttered. "Arien, I wonder if she thinks I'm dead after all this time. I wonder what she'll say. I wonder what the High King will say, when I tell him what I've decided about being High Captain—"

"Halt!" came a voice from above. "What's your business here?"

Mole looked up. Two warriors stood on the ramparts above

the gate, watching him. Neither looked familiar.

"What's your business *there?*" Mole retorted, surprised at being challenged. "There aren't supposed to be guards on the south gate, just a watchman in the high west tower. I'm Captain Moleander, and I was in charge of the guards last winter."

"That was last winter," the sentry returned. "Things have changed."

"What, is there a war on or something? Didn't the High King win his campaign against the sorcerer in Crywyll?"

"Of course, he won," the other sentry said, "and there's no war going on. But there are goblins all around the castle, and all kinds of people mysteriously missing. So we've set guards."

"What did you say your name was again?" the other guard asked.

"Moleander. Captain Moleander."

The two sentries looked at one another. "But you're dead," the first one said. "The High King said so himself. He said something about the *Taran-y-Mor* being lost at sea."

"I suppose it was," Mole said, "but not while I was on it."

The first guard smiled. "Well, then. Lots of people will be glad to see you alive, I'm sure. Let me open the gate for you."

"Please do," Mole said. As soon as the gate cracked open, Mole squeezed through. He didn't stop to talk to the sentries further. He didn't even pause when he passed the stables, though he fancied he heard Wildfoal's whicker. While crossing the common lawn, he kept his face withdrawn in his hood. Although he recognized some of the men at bow practice, he didn't speak to them. He didn't want news of his homecoming to spread before he could find Arien.

Near Arien's room, he broke into a run, flew across the leaves and burst in with a shout.

But the person who started up from the seat by the hearth was not Arien.

Mole frowned, but grinned again. "Fflad!"

"Mole?" Fflad stared at him, then rushed to him, shouting. "Mole!" They gripped each other's shoulders, embraced, pushed back from one another, then began beaming and laughing.

"Mole! I thought you were dead! By the Emperor, I'm glad to see you! I thought you were dead!"

"I came close a time or two," Mole said. "But I'm glad to be back. Fflad! You look so good. You look as if you'd never even been sick!"

"I have," Fflad said, "but I'm better. I was sick until only a few weeks ago. When I recovered, when I was well enough to know what was going on, I learned your ship had disappeared and that you were presumed dead. And I just couldn't forgive myself, because I was the one who sent you to Aelenwaith. By the Emperor, I'm glad to see you back—" The light, however, suddenly drained from Fflad's face as he asked, "Did you find her?"

"Both yes and no," Mole said.

Fflad's eyes flickered. "Tell me."

Mole briefly outlined his experiences in Aelenwaith, how he had searched for Ingra, how he had found the empty house on the mountainside. Fflad listened intently, interrupting only to ask Mole to explain in greater detail. Finally Mole said, "Ingra, I think, is beyond our reach. But I know that Ingra and Escandrin were your parents because of what I saw and what I felt." He reached into his tunic. "And I brought this back for you."

Fflad took the book from Mole, and without lowering his eyes, he opened it. Then when Mole nodded, Fflad looked down and read the penned message several times before looking up again.

"Thank you, Mole," he said. "Thanks for bringing this to me."

"It's not just for you," Mole said, "it's for Arien, too. After all, you two *are* brother and sister, and you should begin sharing things. Now, I haven't walked all this way for nothing. I want to see the look on Arien's face when you tell her about your parents."

Fflad bowed his head. He fingered the book, frowning. "Arien," he murmured, "isn't here."

"Not here? What do you mean? Where is she?"

Biting his lip, Fflad shrugged. "No one knows where she is. A couple of weeks ago she . . . disappeared."

"Disappeared?" Mole seized Fflad's shoulders. "How?"

"We don't know, Mole. We don't have any clue."

"Haven't you searched for her?"

"Of course we have, Mole. Of course we have. Stop shaking me, Mole, so I can explain. About three weeks ago, High Princess Geniolien, Prince Ellari, and Merani all left the castle in the middle of the night. They left a note about having gone on some kind of a quest. A few days later, the day the High

King returned from the west, nobody could find Arien. The High King sent out search parties for all of them, and though they followed one trail—probably Princess Geniolien's—for a long time, they never found any of them. After a few days, the High King called off the search, saying that they'd all come back of their own accord eventually. But none of them have. Berrian and I have been looking for Arien ever since she vanished, and we haven't found any sign at all that she even left the castle. It's very mysterious. We told the High King we couldn't find her trail, and he said she was probably with Geniolien, Merani, and Ellari."

"But she disappeared later than they did!"

"Her disappearance was *discovered* later. But I suppose it is possible she went with the others."

"Arien? Go on a quest? And with Princess Geniolien? Never."

Fflad looked thoughtful, then nodded. "You're right."

Mole turned toward the door. "I'm going to see the High King. I'll ask him to start another search, and if he doesn't, I'll look for her myself. I'm going to find her."

Stopping Mole with a hand on his arm, Fflad objected, "But Mole, you look as if you haven't slept in weeks. You must be starved. At least eat before you go to the High King. You won't find Arien if you collapse from hunger!"

Mole lifted Fflad's hand away. "I'm going to the High King. Go to the kitchens for me, Fflad; have them pack something I can eat on horseback. I'll meet you at the kitchens when I've talked with the king."

Fflad hesitated, but nodding, he vanished out the door.

Mole himself lingered a moment near Arien's hearth, gazing at the ashes in her grate. He picked up a piece of black cloth that hung over a chair and ran his fingers over a strange design of fire and flowers, then put it back on the chair. Arien was all right, he told himself. She had to be. She was just missing—nothing more could be wrong. Nothing.

He loped across the common toward the Royal Quarters. When he came to the bare britches near the feasting hall, he began to sense a hush, like a lull of wind, that made the grey leaves stay still, even when he stepped on them. The sky overhead was shadowed with ropes of clouds, clouds that cast cold shadows over the roofs of the two great halls.

Corridors later, Mole found himself on the balcony of Gion's room, looking over a wilted garden and still pools floating black leaves. Mole didn't both to knock; he threw open Gion's door.

Only dust met his eyes. The windows overlooking the garden were shuttered. A fresh candle on the table lay unscorched. The neat stacks of parchment seemed to be in the same places they had been on the night Mole had last spoken with the High King. Only the medallion was missing, its print visible in the dust on the table.

Mole turned away puzzled, closing the door. Then he hurried from the balcony, making a mental list of all the places the king might be. He hurried down empty halls, through empty gardens, across empty bridges. He saw no one. The gilded doors of the king's personal chambers were locked, as were the gates of the High Princess's garden. The halls of study and the feasting hall were brimming with echoes and dust. Even the common courtyards lay silent.

At last Mole came to the last place on his list, the hall of thrones.

Though Mole expected the doors to be locked, he found them unbolted. A smell of vastness met him when he slipped through the doors, a smell that reminded him of the burned ends of candles. It was very cold, even though the afternoon light edged through tall windows to light the hall. Dust and sunglow obscured the high dais at the end of the room, where stood the seven stone thrones of the kingdoms; these were used, under normal circumstances, only during coronations or great councils of war.

The High King sat in the great throne, garbed in royal blue, with the crown of Llarandil in his lap. In all Mole's years at Drallm, he had seen the high crown only once, and from a much greater distance than he saw it now. Bright in itself, the crown sparkled with pea-sized jewels that cast a glittering web of light on the face of the king.

His skin prickling, Mole bowed. He said, "Your Majesty."

The High King looked up, but he was too far away for Mole to see his face. "Yes," the king said, "what do you want?"

Mole took a step forward. "Sire. It's me, Captain Moleander."

"Oh, Moleander," Gion called. "I didn't recognize you in those clothes, and with the sun in my eyes." The king absently touched the highest jewel of the crown. "Come nearer, Moleander. I'm glad to see you didn't drown with the *Tarany-Mor*."

Mole didn't move nearer. "Arien is missing," he said. "Where could she be?"

The High King shrugged. "Her loss was unfortunate," he said, tapping his fingers on the crown. "But I assure you she isn't in the castle, nor within many miles of it."

Mole's throat went dry.

"I see," the High King resumed, "that you've come to me unarmed. A becoming visit for royalty, but less becoming for you. You do look better with Sodrith at your side than with that empty belt." For the first time the king shifted; he put the crown aside and leaned forward. "Tell me," he said, "where is the Sword?"

Mole cringed at the fire he saw in the king's eyes.

"Where is the Sword?" the king repeated.

Mole stepped back. *"You* have it, don't you?"

The king reclined into his throne. "The air is thick, Captain Moleander," he said. "I seem to have forgotten. Do I, in fact, have your Sword?"

Mole narrowed his eyes. "I gave it to you, because I didn't want to take it to Aelenwaith. I gave it to you because I didn't want to be High Captain. I still don't, but I'd like to be a captain still, if it's all right with you." The High King still looked blank. "Don't you remember the night I came to your study and left the Sword with you?"

"Yes," Gion said, "the study. Then it will be there still?"

"You said you'd put it in safekeeping."

The High King laughed. "Oh yes, I did. Captain Moleander, I'm not feeling myself this afternoon. My memory is dim. Maybe you should leave."

"But what about the Sword? And what about Arien?"

"If you want to look for Arien, you'll have to organize your own search. I can't spare any warriors for you. I'm very sorry, but it's true. You see, this business with Branddabon isn't quite over yet."

Branddabon slipped from a practiced tongue.

"About your Sword," the High King went on, "I'm having such an awful time with my memory. I mentioned that already, didn't I? I'm sure, though, that I'll be able to remember where I put it soon. Come back tomorrow, will you?"

Mole nodded. He walked back toward the doors. The sun was low in the windows now; it made the hall seem to glow in scarlet.

"Good-bye, Your Majesty," Mole said at the door.

Mole heard the reply just before the door closed behind him. "Good-bye."

SAGA SIX

• 8 •

The Night of Cloaks

THEY CAME, ONE by one. Seeming to detach themselves from the darkness as the glow from the shuttered windows struck them, they knocked furtively at the door. They seemed to shrink back from the door as it opened, like night creatures unaccustomed to light. A chill from the night clung to their cloaks as they came into the room, but they did not warm themselves at the hearth. They sat silently at the table and kept their hoods tightly drawn.

Berrian nodded as they came in, for he had predicted to Mole that only the young captains would come. Eheran, Paladain, Fendwr, and Celain, the captains nearest Mole's age, appeared, but none of the older captains or lords arrived. The only older man came with Fflad; he was Gwael, the Chief Minstrel, and he looked at Mole with stone-cold eyes as he took his seat.

Somehow Mole knew no more would come. He slid the bolt across the door, peered out the shutters, then moved to the table. He felt eyes watching him from the hoods. The fire at his back felt hot even before he began to speak.

"Thank you, all of you, for coming."

"You can thank us best," Gwael said, "by telling us why you summoned us. Your message was brief and mysterious. It smelled of treachery."

"As well it might," Mole said, "for there is treachery, though none to be made by me. That's why you're all here. A terrible thing has happened. I ask you first to believe that it has happened, then to help me fight against it."

"War?" Paladain asked, pushing back his hood. "Is it war?"

"No, it's far more terrible than that. In war you have an enemy to fight, and you know who is an enemy."

"We don't understand you," Fendwr murmured. "Tell us what's wrong."

"Yes," Berrian said, grimly, "tell them."

Mole swallowed; his words stuck in his throat. He said at last, "The High King is not the High King." He looked from one captain to the next; he read both disbelief and indignation in their faces. He went on before any of them could protest. "I visited a man this afternoon who sat in the High King's throne and wore his body. But the man wasn't the High King. He wasn't Gion."

"But that's impossible," Celain burst out. His fists met the table. "Those of us who followed the High King to war in Crywyll know that the man you're talking about is the same man you left when you went to Aelenwaith. Moleander, he hardly left our side—"

"He must have," Mole said, teeth set, "for he isn't here at Drallm."

"Of course he is," Fendwr said. "We've all seen him."

Paladain silenced the others with a sweep of his hand. "Let Moleander talk. If he thinks the man isn't Gion, he must have his reasons. You do, don't you, Mole?"

Mole nodded. "I've known the High King for more than two years," he said, "but I've never known him to sit in the great throne all by himself, with the crown of Llarandil in his lap. And he was in the hall of thrones when his study hasn't been used in weeks, even months. That's just not like him."

"You mean," Gwael said, "that's not how he *used* to be. People change, Moleander. You've changed yourself since you left for Aelenwaith. But none of us are accusing you of being an imposter."

"But people don't change that much," Mole said. "And people don't suddenly forget who you are. When I came into the hall of thrones, he didn't even recognize me. And he didn't remember that I had given him Sodrith for safekeeping. And he was very interested—preoccupied, even—with the Sword."

"If he isn't the High King and didn't recognize you, why does he recognize all of us?"

Mole threw up his hands. "How should I know? I'd guess, though, that when he first came, he kept someone near at hand who knew all of you, until he had mastered all your names. But he was alone when I spoke with him, alone and unprepared. And he didn't know me or remember any of the things the High King would remember."

No one spoke. A few of the captains looked at Mole, but most of them watched the fire, fists under their chins. "I have noticed that the High King hasn't been quite himself," Paladain said, with effort. "The whole ride back from Crywyll he was very curt with me. Usually he's friendly. But I thought it was only because he was tired."

"He may still be tired," Celain countered, sitting up straight. "He may be going mad, even. But will we help him by plotting against him, by rubbing salt into his wounds?"

"But the man isn't the High King, I tell you. I *know.*"

"Very well, then," Fendwr said, "if the man we see isn't High King Gion, who is he?"

"And what's happened to the real High King?" Celain added.

"The real High King," Mole said, "is dead. And I think I stumbled on the place where he's buried." He told them of the grave he had found under the alder trees, of the flowers growing on it, and of the tracks he had seen indicating a hasty burial by men from the sea. "The person who is responsible for the secret murder of the High King is the same person who took his shape."

Fflad and Berrian said together, "Branddabon."

"But that's nonsense!" Celain stormed, rising to his feet. "I saw him killed myself, on the bank of the River Ystadun."

"You *thought* you saw him killed, you mean."

"Sorcerers are masters of deceit and appearance," Berrian said. "The man you saw die, Celain, was no more the sorcerer Branddabon than the man among us is High King Gion."

Paladain stood up beside his brother, but he waited till everyone was watching him before he spoke. "I can't speak for any of the rest of you, but it's plain to me that the High King is an imposter."

Celain grimaced. "It is not plain!"

"It's plain that we've got to do something to find out," Berrian retorted. "That's the very least we can do."

"But how?" Celain demanded.

Flames chattered in the silence that followed.

"I know," Fflad said, features crimson, "we can use the Binding Ring of Merwnedd on him."

Mole smiled at Fflad. "I thought of that, but I'm afraid it won't work. If Branddabon had the power to change his shape, he must have the power to manipulate such a device as your binding ring. Besides, Gion's only relative, Princess Geniolien, is missing."

"I've got an idea," Eheran said. "We can kidnap him and put him in the dungeon until we get the truth from him. After all, he is here in Drallm, and Drallm's still our castle."

Mole considered, but only for a moment. "Too dangerous," he said. "We don't know whether Drallm is still *our* castle. We don't know how much power Branddabon has or how many of his men he's substituted for ours. And if we try to imprison the High King, we can't tell how many of our good comrades will turn against us to protect him. Also, we don't want to put him on his guard yet. He seems secure now; we don't want to frighten him into doing something rash."

"Besides," Celain added, "what would taking him captive make us if he really is the High King?"

"We're already quite treacherous," Gwael said, drumming his fingers on the table. "Just by coming here, all of us have made ourselves traitors to the High King."

"Only if the High King were the High King," Mole said quickly, "and he isn't."

Paladain moaned, "But how can we know for sure?"

"And how can we expose him if we find out he's an imposter?" Fendwr said.

Mole moved to the fire. "I've got an idea," he said in a low voice. "I didn't want to suggest it as long as there might be another way. But it seems there isn't; we have only one chance. Remember, all of you, that we're not the only ones making plans. Branddabon is plotting, too. What he'll do next we can only guess. But to be prepared for whatever he might do, we've got to gather an army from the kingdoms."

"Muster the kingdoms?" Celain burst out. "Are you mad?"

"It's the only way," Mole said. "It's our only hope. We've got to bring every king in the North to Ranath Drallm. They must come here to judge whether or not the man who claims to be the High King is really Gion—"

"Branddabon won't submit to judgment," Berrian said.

"He doesn't have to, for the plan to work," Mole replied.

"If he does, we have a good chance of proving him an imposter in front of half a dozen kings."

"And if he doesn't?"

"If he doesn't, he will also refuse to let the kings and their armies enter Ranath Drallm. That proves he is an imposter because it breaks the high law. Then we can use the armies of the other kingdoms to liberate Drallm if he tries to hold it against us."

"War," Fendwr murmured, stroking his beard, "and civil war at that. This imposter must be a sorcerer, to think of turning us against ourselves, making us break our swords on our own walls!"

"Yes. This sorcerer is a clever enemy," Mole said. "Maybe too clever."

"Your plan is desperate," Berrian said, after a moment of silence, "but it's sound. I'm with you, Mole."

Paladain pretended to cough. But when he saw the others looking at him, he said, "I'll do whatever you want, Mole."

Another stretch of silence followed, during which the other captains looked at the table, and Celain turned the badge of his captaincy in his fingers. Then, looking at each other, Eheran and Fendwr said, almost at once, "We're in."

"I don't want to be left out," Gwael said in a thick voice. "I don't know if you'll be able to fulfill your plots, but I'll do what I can for you."

All of them turned to Celain, whose head was down. But when he looked up, his eyes flamed and his lips were pinched with fury. "What?" he snarled, "have all of you crowned Moleander the new king? Are you all so easily used by him? Even if a sorcerer sits on the high throne, who is Moleander Ammarbane to take charge of the war!"

Mole opened his mouth, but he had no chance to answer, for Berrian stepped in front of him, hand on his sword. "Moleander was to be made High Captain!"

"*To be*," Celain sneered. "What is *to be*."

"Closer than you," Fendwr said. "Are you jealous when so much is at stake?"

"So much *is* at stake. *So much!* If we're to do this thing, it's got to be done right. Who is Moleander to command us?"

"Celain!" Paladain shouted, "hold your tongue!"

"No," Mole said, holding his arm up for silence, "no, let him question me. He's wise to ask who I am to lead you. Let me tell you. My duty to all that is good is my authority." He thought of the staff. "There is no more, but no less. I'm like a thorn on the branch with a rose; I have grown only to protect the rose, not to be beautiful, not to be powerful. No one can question my existence or why it is my task to prick the fingers of any force that wants to destroy the flower—"

"I don't want nonsense," Celain growled, "I want an answer. Who are you take the affairs of all the kingdoms on your shoulders? Who are you?"

"I am Moleander," Mole said. "I am Briarborn, holder of the staff, bearer of the Sword of Speech. I am Ammarbane, killer of the Black Counselor, foe of all sorcerers. I am son of thorn and brother of briar. I am a captain who has seen evil and who pleads that you help him."

Grimacing, Celain searched Mole's face, then looked at the others, all of whom had stood up while Mole spoke. He shuddered.

"Very well," he said. "I'll help."

Mole still felt warm in his cheeks. He sighed. "Good. I'll need all of you. We've got to move quickly, tonight if we can."

"Command us," Paladain said, "and we'll do what you say."

"We've got to bring the kings here in all haste. Maybe it would be best for us to split ourselves and ride as messengers to the different strongholds of the kingdoms. Yes, that would be best. Each of you must help persuade a king to bring as large a force as he can muster quickly to someplace near here— let's say the valley of Aedden. It isn't far, north and across the river, because it's an ancient place of good. Yes, tell the kings to bring their guards as secretly as possible, say, within a fortnight."

"Two weeks?" Fendwr said. "A man on a galloping horse can scarcely make it from here to Ranath Sharicom in one. Give us three."

"Three weeks, then. But no longer." Mole looked over the captains. "Now, Berrian, you go to Thrinedor. I'm sure your father will be happy to see you back, happy enough, I hope, that he'll come with you to Aedden. Also, have him send a message by hawk to Fellhaven to have King Daerwyn come with what men he can." Berrian nodded; before Mole had finished, he had donned his cloak. "Fflad, I want you and Paladain to go to Sharicom; talk to Gareth before you talk to his father. Sharicom is the farthest away, so you'll have to take the strongest horses. Also, you may have time to bring only the king, not his army." Mole turned to Eheran and Fendwr. "You two I want to go to Crywyll, *by a northern route.* I don't want you going near where Branddabon's stronghold was. If you can't get King Redwen to come any other way, tell him that Princess Geniolien has agreed to marry his son. Tell him anything. Now, Gwael and Celain, I'd like you to go to the coast cities and to Taranil. You won't find any kings, but you'll find willing warriors."

"What about Aelenwaith?" Eheran asked.

"I'm afraid we'll have to leave Aelenwaith out because we don't have a ship, and the sea is too stormy to cross—"

"Then you're not going to Aelenwaith?" Gwael said. "I thought you'd—"

When Mole shook his head, Celain narrowed his eyes. "Then where *are* you going, Captain Moleander? Or are you going at all?"

Mole stiffened a little; he felt the others watching him expectantly. "No, I'm not going," he said. "I'm staying here."

"But why?"

"It'd be dangerous for you when Branddabon finds out we've gone," Paladain said. "He'll know you're up to something."

"I'm staying here," Mole repeated, "because I want to find out what's happened to Arien. I know that Branddabon had something to do with her disappearance."

"A moment ago you were so selfless, so noble," Celain said, his voice tight again, "and now, while we're galloping across goblin-filled country, *you'll* be hunting for your lady friend."

Mole winced. "That isn't the only reason I'm staying. There's something else I've got to find, something without which we may never be able to defeat Branddabon. I've got to find it or die trying."

Suddenly the others understood. Anger drained from Celain's face.

Berrian said, "The Sword."

A single square of light broke the darkness of the Royal Quarters. A window, no more than a narrow slit of white, high in the wall of the council hall. Creeping in the garden below, Mole fixed his eyes on the light and opened his ears for any sound around him. But except for the crackle of brittle leaves in the wind and a feeble chirp, probably from autumn's last cricket, he heard nothing. He saw nothing but blotted shapes of shrubbery, trees, and lamp posts, none of which were lighted.

Soon the wedge of light glimmered directly over his head, like an odd-shaped moon. Voices, murmuring and distant, peppered the night stillness, losing themselves when the wind gusted. The opening seemed scarcely wide enough to admit a man, and the only way to it was an iron grillwork on which dead ivy climbed. Mole tested it with his hand. It quivered easily. He wasn't sure it would hold his weight, but it was the only way to reach the window without alerting the guards he had glimpsed at the council hall door.

Out of the gloom of the garden Mole climbed. At first the ivy-rack yielded and creaked under his boots. He forced himself to climb more slowly, more silently. One step up. Then, a catlike pause to listen. At last the iron twisted up to the window. Mole stopped. He hooked his elbow over a rung to brace himself. Then he listened.

At first he heard only the buzz of the blood pumping in his temples, but as he waited, he began to hear more. Two voices spoke in the room above, in low tones, away from the window.

". . . a serious complication," said the first voice, whose tone was like the whine of a hungry dog. "Our success depends on secrecy . . ." There was more that Mole could not pick up. "By the Dark One, I curse the sea that brought him back, just as your plan is ripening."

"And the Great Sword unfound," brooded the other voice, one deeper and more chilling. "I planned first to capture it in battle, using one of my guises. But the Sword never came to Crywyll. Then I thought it lost at sea. But now I know it's here, somewhere near."

"A search," the other growled, "a search."

"By the darkness, I've searched already. I can't find it."

"Ask the captain where it is. If he won't tell you freely, turn him over to me, and I'll have Maglaw take care of him . . ." The hiss of the wind erased the rest of what the first voice said.

"But, filth, the boy doesn't know where it is. I should give him to Maglaw anyway, for I think he suspects me; the wretch caught me off-guard. And he asked about the girl. We must have Maglaw make him disappear . . . or die. Only a few know that he's returned."

Reaching to his side, Mole felt no sword. He cursed his lack of preparedness, but waited, locked on the grillwork.

"About the girl," the first voice whined, "maybe she knows something about the Sword. And if not, at least she'll know something about this cursed Moleander and what he's likely to do."

"Bring her. But it won't be easy getting anything out of her. Some power is protecting her. It takes the deepest blood spells to hold her." Mole's body tightened when he heard the first voice call for the guards.

"Bring the girl," the second voice said.

A moment later Mole heard the click of footfalls, the creaking of a door, and a scuffle that lasted for several minutes. It was all he could do to hold himself beneath the window. He told himself that an ill-timed entry might get him killed without helping Arien. He strained his ears.

"Now," the deeper voice said, edged with ice, "I want you to answer this question straight with that crooked tongue of yours, or I'll have Maglaw cut it out for his pleasure. *Where is the Sword?*"

"What sword?" The voice was Arien's, touched with weariness, but still firm with defiance.

"Don't play the fool, filth, or Maglaw will make you into one."

"I don't know. I don't have any idea. And even if I did, do you think I would tell you? You could have that hairy brute of yours torture me all day long, and I wouldn't say a word."

"But you'd scream," the doglike voice said, "you'd scream."

"Oh, you're scum, both of you! You're worse than that *thing* you've got guarding the dungeon. How much longer do you think people will be fooled? I knew you weren't the High King the moment I saw you. Other people will know, too. When he gets back, Mole will know. He's no idiot. *He'll* stop you."

"But he's dead, girl. He drowned at sea. He won't save you. What use is the Great Sword to him now? But think, it can be useful to you. It can buy your life. Tell us where it is."

"I don't know. I said that before."

"We'll give you time to clear your memory, then. You have

one hour. Then we'll bring Maglaw, and if you can't tell us where the Sword is, we'll let him have his way with you."

The creaking of floorboards obscured low, chilling laughter. Finally Mole heard the door close. A bolt fell. Then silence came.

Catching the bottom of the window, Mole swung himself up and vaulted through it. Torches lit a small upper room, and on the floor in one corner, bound with rope, face hidden by hair—Arien.

"Arien!" Mole called. "Arien."

She lifted her head. "Mole! Mole! You're alive! How did you get here? How did you find me?"

"Not so loud," Mole said, kissing her cheek. "Someone might hear us." He set to work on the knots binding her wrists. "And I don't have time to explain." He pulled the first ropes away, tossing them aside. He pushed the circulation back into her wrists with his fingers, keeping his eyes on hers. She began to cry, silently.

He started on her ankles. "Mole, you're alive! They told me you were dead. They all said you'd died in the sea."

Mole lifted her to her feet. "I am alive," he said, "but neither of us will stay alive for long if we stay here. Branddabon and that dog-man will be back soon, and with them that Maglaw. What is it?"

Burying her face in his shoulder, Arien shuddered.

"Never mind," Mole said.

At the window, night hung like a black curtain. Mole kept his eyes on the door. "Are you strong enough to climb down the grating?" he asked.

"Yes, I think so. Mole—"

"Not now. We don't have time. Start down."

He lifted Arien through the window. He heard her grasp the railings, and he backed out the window after her. The rack swayed under their weight, bending like a branch in the wind. To Mole the trip down seemed to be taking an eternity.

Then he heard Arien sigh. She slumped and fell.

Shrubbery splintered. A thump followed as Mole landed beside her and helped her up. She relaxed into his hold. "I haven't eaten much," she explained. "I got a little dizzy on the ladder."

"Are you all right?"

Nodding, she pushed him away and stood erect alone; but

she winced and swayed. Mole took her arm and led her from the garden. "We've got to hurry to the stables," he said.

"We're leaving Drallm?" she asked faintly.

He helped her along, sometimes half-carrying her, until they reached the stables. In the shadow of the stable door, he eased her to a seat against the wall. Promising to return, he slipped into the stable and groped his way to Wildfoal's stall. Stroking the horse's flanks, he whispered, "Quiet, now, steady, boy," as he lifted a saddle from the wall, fitted it across Wildfoal's back, and cinched it beneath his ribs. To be quiet with the harness was more difficult; its trappings tinkled when Mole picked it up and strapped it on Wildfoal's head. The door of the stall squeaked a little as Mole opened it. Then Mole, eyeing the darkness, led Wildfoal to the doors.

Arien waited for him, seemingly only half awake. She sighed as he lifted her to the saddle. "Aren't you going to ride, too?" she asked when she saw him take the rein.

"No. Not yet." He hid a frown. "Not just yet."

As Mole had been promised, the torches above the south gate burned on an empty guard walk. The other captains, with Berrian and Fflad, must have been successful in surprising the gate watch, then scattering into the forest. Hours ago, he guessed. The gate was unbarred, so Mole pushed it open enough to allow himself and Arien to pass.

Outside the gate he hesitated, suddenly torn despite his earlier resolution. Arien slumped over the horse's neck, seeming to doze.

"Arien," he said, touching her arm. "Arien, I want you to promise me something." She looked at him. "I want you to ride to Taranil," he said, "ride as fast as you can, without slowing down, without looking back."

"Mole," she said, clutching his arm, "you're not coming?"

"No." He pulled himself away. "Not now. Not yet. I've got to find the Sword. Arien, promise me."

"I . . . I promise. But Mole—"

He didn't let her finish. Closing his eyes, he shouted for Wildfoal to gallop and slapped the horse's flank. Arien's last words were lost in the clatter of hooves on the road.

Clenching his fists, Mole turned around. He forced his final glimpse of Arien from his mind, pushed through the gate, turned around, and secured the bolt across it.

As he started back into the castle, he saw a shadow shift in the torchlight. He froze. He looked around him, but saw nothing. But before he had taken another step, something crashed across his neck and he fell, cloaked with darkness, to the earth.

• 9 •

Earth Magic

RAVEN CRAG, CATCHING the stony light of the late sun, loomed over the leafless forest. Both its summit and its feet were shrouded in grey mist; between them, against stone cliffs, ravens wheeled, sometimes gliding into the clouds above, sometimes dipping into the trees below.

"I can't understand it," Princess Geniolien said. "He's got to be here somewhere."

"He doesn't *have* to be," Ellari said. "In fact, after two days of searching this barren wood, I'm sure he isn't. Maybe the goblins killed him, or maybe he moved away—"

"But he's too powerful to be bothered by goblins," Geniolien said. She looked off through the trees. "And he's not the kind to move around. And, yes, I'm sure I got my directions right. This is the right place."

Merani sat beside Ellari against an oak stump. "Maybe the Old Man of the Oak isn't real, after all," she said gently. "Maybe we ought to go home before we starve to death." She shivered. "Or freeze to death."

Ellari leaned forward and looked at her. "Merani, if you're cold," he took off his cloak, "put this on."

"That's very kind of you, but I'm all right," she said. "Besides, I wouldn't be any warmer with your cloak if I had to watch the goosebumps grow on your arms like that."

"You're sure?" Ellari asked, still holding out the cloak.

"I'm sure," Merani said, "but thank you."

Reluctantly Ellari put his cloak on again. He fastened the brooch at his throat. "Geniolien," he said, "I think we really can't look for this tree of yours any longer. Snow will begin in a few days, and we're almost out of food."

Geniolien let the wind pull her hair away from her face. She frowned. "I'm afraid you're right."

"It's a shame to come this far for nothing," Ellari said, "but we did our best."

Geniolien bowed her head.

"From what Cwyller's seen," Merani said, "the shortest way out of the mountains isn't the way we came, over the ridges. It's along a ravine that begins just north of Raven Peak and comes out in the foothills, somewhere near Aedden."

"That sounds like a good way," Ellari said. "There are too many goblins the way we came. Besides," he added, glancing at Geniolien, "we can look through this forest one more time on the way out."

Ellari stood up, then helped Merani stand. He took up the packs, weighed them in his arms, and gave the lighter one to Merani. "At least we don't have much to carry," he said. "We'll be able to go faster. We'll be back to the river within a week."

They started out. Their pace, for Geniolien's benefit, was slow, and Merani looked through all the gaps in the trees, although she expected to see nothing. Ellari tried to find a path through the wood they hadn't followed; as a result, Merani found herself squeezing through bracken, bending under low branches, and stepping over logs. But she saw nothing that moved except the twigs in the wind and Cwyller's fleet shape gliding over them. Once or twice Geniolien cried out and pointed to an oak tree, which they all examined thoroughly before proving it to be as ordinary as the rest.

They soon reached the gully. Its rocky sides, thickly wooded, fell sharply away from the rest of the forest. Its bottom seemed stony but clear, as if a stream ran in it during some seasons. They half-walked, half-slid, holding to trees, until they reached the stream bed. It was very quiet in the ravine, and although they saw the wind beating the branches of the trees higher up, they heard nothing below.

Merani was glad to be out of the wind, for even the ring, she was sure, could not keep her skin from reddening with cold and her hair from tangling in her hood. And since Ellari seemed always to be watching her now, she hated to keep brushing it from her eyes.

The ravine was clear and always downhill, so they made good progress. At first Merani marked their movement by the number of side gullies that branched into theirs, but she soon gave up counting. Eventually the ravine became almost a canyon, for stone walls separated them from the forest above.

They had walked only a few miles, however, before the canyon began to widen out and eventually it was as wide as the Thrine. The very tip of Raven Crag arose behind them, and before them a thick oak wood grew between the canyon walls almost without a break. Since there seemed to be no way out of the canyon, and since the wood seemed to thin farther on, Ellari suggested they try to push through.

Passage, however, proved more difficult than they had thought. Branches seemed to move in front of them to bar their way. Roots caught at their feet. Ragged leaves fluttered in their eyes. Ellari had to tug his cloak free from a thornbush. It was a nightmare of shadows and branches until at last they pushed past the final tree into cold sunlight.

Ellari stood, very erect, in front of Merani there. He didn't turn around, even though she called his name. So she waited for Geniolien to come out of the forest, then they both went to Ellari and Merani touched his elbow. He still did not stir.

"Look," he said. "Geniolien, Merani, look!"

A great tree spread in front of them, filling the whole width of the canyon with its boughs. Its crown rose higher than the trees on the canyon rim, but no wind moved its upper branches. Its trunk was so thick that Merani was sure all of them with linked hands could not circle it. Stout branches, all dark and grooved, twisted upward to disappear in clouds of feather-length, rust-colored leaves, many of which trailed downward to give the tree a willow-like appearance. Yet the roots, like thick fingers tearing the earth, told Merani that the tree could be nothing but an oak.

Merani looked at Ellari, then at Geniolien. Geniolien's lips twitched. "Could it be?" she began. But she stopped herself and nodded. Then, leaving the others, she stepped under the nearest branch. Gently she reached up and folded her fingers around a bough. "Derwen," she called, "Old Man of the Oak, hear me. My name is Geniolien Dolengwrydd, High Princess of the kingdoms. I'm of the blood of Llarandil the Great, who first asked a wish from you. I've come all the way from Ranath Drallm to find you."

At first nothing happened, and it seemed to Merani that Geniolien had wasted her breath talking to a large, but otherwise perfectly ordinary tree. Yet Merani, like the princess, waited silently.

It began as a whisper of wind in the very highest part of the tree. It spread like a rumor among the leaves; they shuddered, twitched, shifted, then moved like fingers or tongues. The sigh grew into a noise like the hissing of a storm through a forest. Boughs began to move and creak. Roots seemed to strain against the earth, as if the tree were being pulled upward by some enormous force.

Then the sounds of the tree became a voice, a deep, ponderous voice that was not really a voice at all, merely the breath of the wind in the branches, the tongues of the leaves touching one another, and the groan of the roots in their sockets. The words were very deliberate and slow, so slow that Merani decided they were words only after the first three or four.

"Why . . . have . . . you come?" The sound of the tree, Merani noticed, hauntingly resembled that of an old man laboring to push out words. The very thought of the tree speaking made her skin prickle and her blood run cold. But Geniolien stepped closer.

"We've come to ask a wish of you."

"A wish?" Merani wondered whether the tree, or whatever lived in it, was surprised or angry.

"Yes," Geniolien said. "And I know you've granted wishes before. We've traveled from Drallm to find you, to ask you to use your power, your earth magic, to bind the walls of Ranath Drallm and make them so that nothing, not even goblin fire power, can destroy them."

The tree seemed to need time to absorb all this. "Earth magic . . . can bind," it said, "for a price."

Merani narrowed her eyes at Geniolien. "I told you," she said. "I told you it was all too simple, just to come here and demand a wish. I knew there was a catch to it, Geniolien."

The princess pressed her lips. "What kind of price?"

A minute's pause. "A price," the tree said.

"I really don't know what you mean or what you want from us," Geniolien said, reddening.

"There is always a price," the tree said.

Geniolien blanched. "But we've brought nothing valuable with us," she said. "And I have a feeling that even if we had brought gold or jewels or silver, that's not what you would want. That isn't what you mean by a price, is it?"

"Earth magic needs power," the voice of the tree rumbled, "power."

"I think I know what it means," Ellari said. "Do you remember that part of the verse that said something about roots seeking deep magic pools? That's what it means by a price, I think. I mean, good magic does only good, and evil magic only evil. But earth magic must be something like nature itself, doing both good and evil, but needing some kind of price to do either. It's like something my father once said about planting a new apple tree for every old one we cut down as firewood. It's the same thing."

"Yes," said the tree, "return."

Geniolien sighed. "Of course we ought to pay for what we get. But what does the tree expect us to give it in return for putting a binding spell on the walls of Drallm?"

"I don't have any idea," Ellari said. "Why don't you ask it?"

"All right, Derwen," Geniolien said, "what do you want?"

"Magic," it boomed back, "or life."

Ellari looked at the tree's groping roots. "I think I know what it means by magic: some magical object. But I shudder to think what it means by *life*—"

"It means," Merani said simply, "that it would take one of our lives as payment."

Geniolien grimaced. "Well, that's wholly out of the question. I didn't bring either of you," she nodded at Ellari and Merani, "to have some tree draw the life out of you. We can't spare any of our lives, and since we don't have anything magical to give, I suggest we leave at once."

After hesitating for a moment, Merani said, "Wait!"

Geniolien looked at her. "No, Merani. I know what you're going to say, but you're mad to say it. Of course I want the walls of Drallm to be bound, but not badly enough to lose you."

"I'm not offering my life," Merani said, feeling the blood rush to her face. "I'm offering something else." Geniolien and Ellari looked at her, and it seemed that a branch of red leaves leaned nearer. "I'm offering the oak something magical." Bowing her head, Merani thrust up the ring.

"That ring," Ellari said, blankly, "is magical?"

"Very," Merani replied. She turned to the tree, holding the ring within reach of the leaves. "Is this payment enough for Geniolien's wish?"

A few leaves fluttered, and the nearest root seemed to stretch. "Yes," the tree answered, "it is payment enough."

"But Merani," Ellari asked, "what is it?"

"And where did you get it?" Geniolien added.

Merani twisted the ring on her finger, not really wanting to take it off. "I found it in the goblin lair," she said.

"In the goblin lair?" Geniolien frowned. "Why didn't you tell us?"

"What does it do?" Ellari said, looking at her sidelong. "Does it make you disappear or see in the dark or what?"

For an answer, Merani took off the ring. At once the skin on her hand reddened and freckled, her nose felt sunburned, and threads of orange hair fell on her shoulders. She watched Ellari note the change; he seemed bewildered, like a man awakened from a pleasant dream. Geniolien frowned and said, "Why didn't you tell us?"

Because Ellari was looking at her, Merani couldn't answer. But a gleam in her eye, possibly the reflection of the ring, betrayed her, and pressing his lips in sudden understanding, Ellari turned away from her.

"Are you sure you want to give up the ring?" Geniolien said, her face soft again. "After all, it's my wish and your ring."

Merani closed her eyes. "I don't want it anymore," she said. "I was foolish to use it in the first place, for I'm a warrior not a lady, and my luck is with hawks and arrows, not with needles and princes." She raised her head to the tree. "How do you want me to give you the ring?"

"Throw it," the tree answered, "into my branches."

Merani tossed the ring, but it scarcely reached the lowest branches because she hesitated at the last moment. She expected it to fall to the ground, but instead it sparkled among the leaves and vanished. Nothing dropped from the tree's low boughs.

"There, now, Geniolien," Merani said, slapping the dust from her hands. "Make your wish, and let's be on our way."

"Derwen," Geniolien said to the tree, "how do I make my wish?"

"Take a leaf," the tree said, "wish on it. Then bury it." The tree seemed to lean a branch down to within Geniolien's reach. "Then the wish will be bound."

Geniolien took hold of a leaf and plucked it from the branch. The whole tree seemed to shake for a moment afterward. She held the leaf in her hand, and when the disturbance had stopped, she pressed it between her palms. "By the power of earth magic," Merani heard her say, "I command that the walls of Ranath Drallm be bound stone on stone from now to the end of time." Then Geniolien knelt down, pushed the soft earth away with her hands, folded the leaf into the pocket she had made, then covered it again with dirt.

Standing up, she sighed and faced Merani and Ellari. In spite of the soil on her knees, she smiled. "We can go home, now," she said.

For the rest of the day, they followed the canyon out of the mountains. Beyond the great oak, the canyon became narrower again, and its walls steeper and higher. A few trees grew on the bluffs above, and a few in the bottom of the canyon. A spring about a mile below the oak's clearing created a little brook, swift and noisy, which rushed between stands of spindly, leafless trees.

None of them spoke. Merani withdrew into her hood, talking only to Cwyller. Ellari did not speak at all; he kept his head high and his arms folded and did not look at either Geniolien or Merani. For her part, Geniolien simply smiled vaguely as they walked along.

Since Cwyller had seen nothing out of the ordinary, they decided to build a fire in the grove where they planned to spend the night. Ellari took his leave of them earlier than was his custom; he climbed high through the trees, as far as the canyon wall, to sleep. Merani and Geniolien were left to tend the coals of the dying fire, which cast bone-colored light on the undersides of the branches.

"You did want to keep that ring, no matter what you said," Geniolien said. "I shouldn't ever have let you give it up."

"I wanted to give it up," Merani said, staring at the fire. "It was hard to, but I wanted to. I couldn't stand being . . . *fake* any longer. You know what Ellari said about there being a price for everything magical? He was right. I paid with ugliness, ugliness Ellari saw in me when he realized I had used the ring to deceive him." Merani paused and began poking at the ashes with a stick. "Now, most likely, he'll never speak to me again. He'll never even look at me again."

Geniolien sighed. "Price applies to things that aren't magical, too," she said. "I owe you for giving up your ring to pay for *my* wish. I'll tell you what. *I'll* talk to Ellari for you, explain that you didn't mean any harm, that you used the ring unintentionally."

"But that's just it," Merani moaned. "I *didn't* use the ring unintentionally. I used it to make Ellari look at me. And he knows it."

"If it comes to that, I don't see what's so wrong about you wanting him to look at you. It sounds perfectly natural to me. After all, other girls arrange their hair and sew new gowns to make men notice them. I don't see that your ring was any different."

"But it *was* different," Merani said. "Maybe because it was magic. But maybe because I was never supposed to be beautiful."

"But you are beautiful!" Geniolien said.

"Not to Ellari. Not anymore."

"What, is Ellari the only person on earth? Is he the only person you've ever liked? Look, Merani, look at the stars coming out over the mountains. See how many there are? Dozens. Hundreds. Thousands. There are that many men in the world, at least. And one of them will be someone you'll like just as much as Ellari, and he'll like you, not because of some magic ring, but because of the way you shoot your bow, the way you can talk to Cwyller, and the way you keep your head no matter what's going wrong."

"It's going to be dark tonight," Merani remarked, pretending to stifle a yawn. "The clouds are covering up the stars."

The next five days were the most miserable of Merani's life. It wasn't because of the cold, though frost patterned their cloaks each morning and ice-crusted pools bordered the brook. It wasn't because of the walking and the load she carried, even though they followed the canyon from dawn till dusk. And it wasn't even because she had lost the ring, though she dreamed of it every night, worn on the hand of a beautiful girl with a hawk on her shoulder. She was miserable because Ellari, who had ignored her before, began to ignore her again. At first he forced himself to do so; he kept his eyes averted from hers and frowned when she looked at him. But his sullen mood lifted after a day or so, and he began to speak freely with Princess Geniolien. He spoke to Merani as well, but just as he had before, only to ask her where Cwyller was or whether a lump of stone on the cliff might be a goblin.

At least he should hate me, Merani thought. I'd rather be hated than forgotten. But the nature of the ring, she decided, was such that the attention it had earned for her vanished when it was gone.

Yet after hours of dark reflection, Merani made herself two promises. The first was that she would never use anything magical again, at least not without determining what it might do to her. The second was that she would never try to deceive herself or others. She would never try to be anything she was not.

On the evening of the fifth day, Merani downed a running rabbit with an arrow. "I've never seen anyone shoot a bow as well as you do," Ellari said while Merani removed the arrow, rinsed it off in the brook, and replaced it in her quiver. "Remind me to stay on your side in case of a battle."

Merani smiled. Before, this kind of praise from Ellari had only vexed her. But now it was enough. "Thank you," she said. "It's not hard, you know. If you have time when we get back to Ranath Drallm, I'll be happy to teach you."

The sixth day was better. The clouds promised snow, and the three had almost nothing in their packs for breakfast, but all of them woke up with smiles. The canyon walls began to widen by noon; by afternoon the walls gave way altogether, and they struck off northward across sage-covered hills in hope of finding Aedden, from which, Geniolien said, it would be easy to reach the River Thrine and thereby Drallm.

Just as a winterlike dusk set in, they came to the summit of a line of stony hills running east and west. Below spread a broad, low valley, flat and grassy. Shreds of cloud, speckled with the sunset, hung against the hills on the far side of the valley.

"This must be Aedden," Geniolien said when she saw it.

Ellari hooked his fingers in his belt. "It's beautiful, at least

after the rugged country we've been through. It looks like the
kind of land that in Thrinedor makes good orchards."

"There were fields here once," Geniolien replied. "Aedden
of old was the seat of High King Llarandil. There was a castle
here, surrounded by pastures full of sheep. But the castle—no
one even remembers its name, now, if it had one—fell to ruin
in the days after Llarandil's death. The last stones were broken
to dust in the goblin wars. But this place is still a stronghold
of good. Can't you feel it?"

Merani sniffed the wind. "There's something, something in
the wind from across the valley. But it doesn't smell like good-
ness. It smells like smoke. Wood smoke. Wait. Here comes
Cwyller. Maybe he's seen something."

"Whether he has or not, I've seen something," Ellari said.
He squinted into the mist-smudged twilight. "There, against
those far hills. Like stars. I think it's fires, dozens of them."

Looking where Ellari pointed, Merani saw scattered points
of light near the feet of the north hills, twinkling a little through
the mist. They were too red to be anything but campfires,
maybe bonfires. She caught Cwyller on her arm and listened
to him. "They're men, not goblins," she said. She paused to
listen again. "Many of them, more than Cwyller's seen since
the Battle of Rathvidrian. And horses. And weapons. And
kings—I know that because Cwyller saw hawks."

Listening to Cwyller's chatter, Ellari made a face. "You
understand all that, Merani? Do you understand his language?"

"I understand Cwyller." Merani said. "I understand how he
reacts to things. It isn't anything more than that."

Ellari smiled. "Whatever you do, it's really amazing."

"Never mind Cwyller," said Geniolien, who had taken several steps down the hill. "What about that war camp? Look,
you can see lights all up and down that side of the valley.
What's going on?"

"Does it really matter as long as they aren't goblins?"

"Yes, it does matter. It could be a sorcerer's army."

"It isn't," Merani said. "Cwyller would have seen sorcerers.
But he didn't. He saw only kings and warriors."

Genilien bit her finger. "But that's almost as bad," she said.
"It means that someone's going to war. It means that something
went wrong back in Crywyll."

"Then what are they doing here?" Ellari asked.

"That's what I want to find out," Geniolien said. Without

waiting to see if the others would follow her, she started down the hill and across the meadow. Ellari and Merani looked at one another, read differing ideas in each other's face, then hurried to catch up with Geniolien.

As they crossed the valley, Merani could scarcely see the deep winter-white grass through which they walked. But though she could not see where she was stepping, she could see the lights of fires ahead of her, strung up and down the valley, some of them near enough that she could see flames and fire-light and men crouching near them.

"By the Emperor," Ellari said, "your hawk was right. There's a whole army here. Or several. I didn't know there were this many men in all the Kingdoms."

"But what are they *doing* here?" Geniolien said. "Who are they planning to attack? There aren't any evil strongholds in this part of the country, and there are too many of them to be goblin hunting."

"Unless the goblins have taken a city," Ellari suggested, "one of the coastland cities like Taranil."

"Then they would gather at Drallm, not here," Geniolien pointed out.

It grew colder, though the wind seemed warmer because of the smoke. Merani found that, consciously or otherwise, Geniolien was leading them toward the center of the camp, toward the brightest concentration of watchfires, and a particularly large fire around which a crowd had gathered. Merani saw spears set up around it, spears bearing wind-teased banners that at first she couldn't identify.

"Wait!" she said at last. "Maybe mist or smoke has gotten into my eyes, but one of those banners looks like the standard of the House of Vivrandon."

"I was just going to say," Ellari said in a low voice, "that one of those flags looks like the one my father takes to battle."

"I can't see either of the ones you mean," Geniolien said, "but I see the colors of Crywyll on the far side of the fire. Red and brown. Who ever is here, I hope Prince Redwar isn't."

They had begun to run but were still far from the fire when a horseman swept out of the darkness. He wore a tall helmet and carried a long spear, which he thrust into the earth in front of them. "Who are you?" he demanded. "And what are you doing in Aedden?"

Drawing his sword, Ellari threw it up against the spear. "Be careful who you ride down," he shouted back. "I'm Ellari, prince of Thrinedor, and with me is High Princess Geniolien!"

"And Merani Felleira," Merani added, "who almost put an arrow through you when you came charging at us like that!"

The rider stiffened in his saddle. "Whether you're who you claim to be or not, I can't say, but at least you don't seem to be goblins. I'm sorry to surprise you, but what was I to think when I saw you running in the dark? If you want to talk to the kings, they're in council right now. You shouldn't bother them."

"But one of the kings is my father!" Ellari burst out. "He may want to whip me for what I've done, but I'm sure he'll want to see me—"

"The High King," Geniolien interrupted, "is he here?"

"You *must* be the Princess to ask a question like that," the rider said. "Maybe you'd better go to the council fire, after all. Follow me. I'll take you there."

"I don't like this," Geniolien said as they hurried along. "Something's wrong here. With all these kings, the High King ought to be here. If he isn't, there's more than smoke in the wind."

"Treachery?" Ellari hazarded. "You can't mean that."

"I hope not," Geniolien answered. "But if it is, Ellari," she went on, "I'm afraid you and I are on different sides."

They didn't speak any more. Merani felt a knot in her stomach; she exchanged glances with Ellari as the council fire loomed ahead. Soon the rider peeled away to gallop into the darkness, and the three found themselves on the edge of the firelight.

Logs, used as benches, ringed the fire. On them sat several dozen men, talking above the sounds of the blaze. Merani immediately recognized almost all the people on the far side. She saw Ellari's father, King Ellarwy of Thrinedor, grim-faced, and Prince Berrian at his side. She saw in the back young captains whose faces were lost in shadow. She saw someone who looked a lot like Arien sitting next to a man who could only be Fflad. And more faces were familiar, so many that Merani almost thought the firelight was deceiving her. Yet none of the faces were as she remembered them; all were creased with unhappiness, impatience, and grief.

A tall, dark man, whom Merani recognized as King Cashma of Sharicom, was speaking when they approached. ". . . All we can hope to do is besiege Ranath Drallm, take it, and slay the man who claims to be the High King—"

"Wait!" Geniolien pushed through the crowd to the side of the fire. Her eyes burned. "Wait," she said again, in a voice both broken and firm. "If all of you are going to slay the High King," she said, "you'd better kill me first."

• 10 •

Winter Fires

"WHY, IN HWYL'S name, would we want to kill you?" said King Ellarwy, storming to his feet. He reached the High Princess, and before she could stop him, he took her arm in his hand. "Your Majesty, you've been lost for a very long time and things have changed. We don't plan to kill your brother."

"I heard you," Geniolien said. "You said you were going to kill the High King in Drallm. And my brother is High King."

"Father," Ellari said, breaking into the circle. "How can you talk such treason? And if you try to harm Princess Geniolien—"

"Harm Princess Geniolien?" King Ellarwy bellowed. "Ellari! If it isn't enough for you to appear out of nowhere when I think you're dead, you accuse me of treason and of trying to harm the High Princess. By Hwyl, boy, the princess is High Queen now; technically, at least. And I'll have no talk of treason out of you. There's been enough argument about treason all these weeks. But there's none of it now, not since the man who pretends to be High King has refused our demands and has locked up Ranath Drallm against us!"

Ellari went pale. "I don't understand."

"I don't either." Geniolien glanced around the circle, frowning. "I don't know what you mean, callimg me High Queen and telling me that my brother's pretending to be High King and breaking the high law. That can't be. I think all of you are trying to confuse me!"

130

"Father," Berrian said, touching King Ellarwy's shoulder, "I think you're not helping the princess to understand. And it won't do any good to shout at Ellari. He's been gone, too, you know."

"Yes," King Ellarwy said, glaring at Ellari, "I know."

"Princess," Berrian said softly, leading her a little way from the others, "this camp isn't what it seems to be. We're not doing what we seem to be doing. We're all in great danger from an evil that's more powerful than we thought. My father's a little nervous—he's always bad-tempered when he goes to war. And he was surprised to see you. I hope you'll forgive his bluntness. It *was* a shock to us when you appeared."

"Prince Berrian," Geniolien said, "you aren't making any more sense than your father."

Berrian bowed his head. "That's because," he murmured, "that's because I don't want to be the one to tell you your brother Gion is dead."

"Dead!" Geniolien exclaimed, looking around at the faces of the kings. "But that's not possible."

"We're quite sure now," Berrian said. "He died in Crywyll, in the war. But the sorcerer Branddabon wore his shape back to Ranath Drallm and has pretended to be the High King ever since."

"But how do you know? How did you find out?"

"Mole found out," Arien said. She stood up. "He's the one who sent for all the kings."

Geniolien looked around her. "Moleander. Captain Moleander? Where is he?"

"We don't know," Berrian replied, looking at the ground. "He stayed in Ranath Drallm after the rest of us left, to look for his Sword. But no one has heard of him since—"

Geniolien lifted hands to her cheeks. "How can I believe someone who isn't even here?"

"Believe me," Arien said. "I saw the High King, too, and he wasn't your brother. If you'd seen him, you'd have known, too."

"Your brother was a great High King," King Cashma said, "and he will be remembered as long as these kingdoms last."

"But accept the fact that he's dead, Your Majesty," King Ellarwy said. "Join us to avenge his death. We can't afford not to have you on our side."

Covering her mouth with her hand, Geniolien nodded slowly.

"Yes, yes. I think I must believe you. And I'll do what I can to help. But let me get used to it first."

"You are, of course, your brother's heir," King Redwen said from across the fire. "But right now, we're on the brink of war, a terrible war, and if you don't mind, we kings will run things until we've defeated Branddabon."

"We've chosen King Ellarwy of Thrinedor to be our commander for the time being," King Daerwyn of Vivrandon said, "because he at least has the blood of Llarandil in him."

Merani, who had been watching all that had happened from beyond the ring of light, decided that enough had been said. Geniolien needed time to think, to really realize what had happened. So she pushed her way to Geniolien and took the princess's arm. "I'm sorry about your brother," she said, hardly daring to meet Geniolien's eyes. "I liked him. He was always as kind to me as you've been. But now we must find a seat, somewhere in the back. These kings must plan what is to be done." Merani guided Geniolien to a seat beside Arien, who whispered soemthing in Geniolien's ear that Merani couldn't hear. Ellari started to follow them, but King Ellarwy glared at him, so he sat down next to Berrian.

"I'm glad we mentioned Mole," Berrian said, "because I think we should consider him in our plans. He could make the difference between victory and defeat for us."

"One man?" King Redwen said incredulously. "Surely not!"

"It's not just Mole," Fflad said, "it's the Sword. Together they've slain two sorcerers. If Branddabon has protected his life with sorcery, Mole's Sword may be the only thing that can kill him—"

"Yes," Prince Gareth said, looking at Fflad, "we should wait for Mole."

"We can't afford to wait for Mole any longer," King Ellarwy said, "even though he would be useful to us. There's the smell of snow in the air. And mischief. The longer we wait, the more prepared for our attack Branddabon will be—"

"But what about Mole?" Berrian persisted. "He may be on his way."

"If he's on his way," King Ellarwy replied, "we'll meet him as we march to Drallm. If he's being held prisoner at Drallm, we can help him most by liberating it. And I'm afraid there's nothing we can do for him if he's . . ." King Ellarwy's voice trailed off; instead of finishing, he watched a pair of warriors lift another log onto the fire.

"All of us agree that we've got to attack Drallm soon," King Daerwyn said. "Now that we know the High King is an imposter, we can carry out the plans we've already discussed. The only thing that still bothers me is the people—like Mole—who are still in Ranath Drallm. Will they realize the High King isn't Gion, or will they fight for him—against us? I don't mind killing goblins and traitors. But what about those Branddabon has fooled?"

"That's the evil in this sorcerer's plan," King Ellarwy said. "He wants us to turn against ourselves. But we've got to take Drallm and kill the sorcerer. We'll just have to hope that not too many of those who are loyal to the real High King are hurt or killed."

"In battle," King Redwen muttered, "it's not easy to be particular about who you kill."

"Now," King Ellarwy said, "if all of you agree, I think we ought to march for Drallm tomorrow. I know that's soon. But we can't waste time. Foul weather's brewing—that's a gift from Branddabon, I'm sure. Now I suggest that most of us get some sleep. Daerwyn, Redwen, Cashma; I want to speak with you in my tent. We ought to map out the particulars of our battle plans tonight."

Mole lay in darkness, on his stomach, on some kind of rough bench, with his arms dangling to touch cold stone. His mind was numb; thirst lay sharp in his throat; and pain made his jaw tighten when he tried to lift his head. He couldn't tell how long he had been lying there, or whether he had been asleep or awake or neither. He had no idea of where he was or how he had been brought here, except for a few flash memories of torchlit catacombs and lumbering shadows.

When he tried to lift his head again, his mind began to buzz. But pain, burning up and down his back, cleared away some of the prison of darkness, shedding light on memories he didn't want of the huge, deformed shape of Maglaw. He heard again the whip hissing above him, cracking across his back.

"I don't know!" he found himself shouting. "I don't know where it is!"

But there was no black questioner now, no lash of the whip.

Mole forced his body to relax back onto the bench and stared into blackness. "I don't know where the Sword is," he heard himself whisper, "and if I did, I wouldn't tell you." The shadow of a whip licked across his imagination, but he pinched his eyes closed to block it out.

Weeks, he thought suddenly. I've been here, in this nightmarish hole, for weeks. He wondered whether any of the kings had gathered or whether Branddabon had acted before they could, turning the world into darkness with some great and abominable spell.

The Book of Gath, Mole thought, what if the sorcerer had found the Book in the vaults of Drallm? With a single charm from its pages, he could turn the world into a whirlwind of black fire.

And what if he had found the Sword? If he had, Mole realized, there would have been no sense in keeping him alive to torture him. The thing Maglaw would have been given its way with him—

Mole shuddered. "No!" he said aloud, wincing, "No!"

He had to think of something pleasant, he knew. He had to have something to grasp to keep the darkness from driving him mad. He tried to remember Arien, to recall the details of her face; but her memory was fleeting, disjointed, and the only firm picture he could get of her was her face, pale in the moonlight, pocked with dirt and tears. Perhaps that was the face she had worn more than four years before when she had found he had crossed the river to challenge Ammar, leaving her alone.

But Ammar was dead.

Shaking his head, Mole tried to sit up. He forced himself partway up, then collapsed under a wave of weakness and pain. He gritted his teeth and strained up again, grunting and panting until he was at last sitting up. The darkness filled with flecks of minute light, but as his head cleared, all went black again. Nightmares closed in on him, but he shoved them away until he could think clearly.

He must escape. The realization struck him like a shaft of light, and he wondered why he had not tried it before. If he had, he couldn't remember. And if he hadn't, what had kept him from trying?

Falling to his knees, he began to grope. His hand clattered on something metal. A water tray. He buried his fingers in it, but found only dust. He suddenly remembered having drunk bitter water from the dish between episodes of questioning, and he wondered whether its dryness meant that his captors had given up on him or had been drawn away from the dungeons by something more vital than finding the Sword. Whatever, if it meant that they would not come back, Mole was grateful in spite of his hunger and thirst. He would escape.

His cubicle, he found after a short investigation, was little more than the height of a man in any of its dimensions. Its walls and floor seemed to be made of cemented stone. A metal door on one side was barred, presumably, from the outside; in it was a tiny grate through which Mole remembered having seen the glint of Maglaw's fangs.

If he was in a deep trove or dungeon, he reasoned, he could not hope to escape by working stones loose. His only hope was the door and the black corridor beyond. And his only hope of breaking through the door was to surprise someone who opened it, a slim possibility considering his weakness, or somehow break or remove the latch outside.

He felt around for some tool. He himself had been stripped of everything but a pair of cloth trousers. Quickly he searched his cell again, but found nothing more than a stale crust of bread, which he ate, and the water tray, which he kept in his hands when he sat down on the bench again. The dish, though rough and heavy, had a tapering rim more than two thornbreadths across. The idea came to him suddenly that if he slipped the rim into the crack at the side of the door, he might be able to knock loose the bolt outside. He rushed to the door and knelt, fingers throbbing, to insert the rim. At first he thought the edge of the plate wouldn't fit, but at last he forced it in. He moved it up, then down. It moved freely, making a sound like a sword rubbing against its sheath. At the center of the crack it met something that clanked. Bringing the dish down a little, Mole shoved the rim as far into the door as it would go, then thrust it upward violently. Something outside the door clattered; echoes of the noise pulsed through the darkness.

Biting his lip, hardly daring to breathe, Mole pushed against the door. Nothing happened. He threw his shoulder against the door. Still it did not yield. Staggering to his feet, he fell against the door, but it only boomed like laughter and remained, fast and closed, in the stone doorway. In sudden giddiness, Mole grasped the bars of the window and slumped away from it.

With a thin squeak, it opened inward. Dropping to his knees, Mole blinked into the darkness. An earthy draft, smelling of iron and torchsmoke, curled through the door. When it met his shoulders, he shivered. He stood up then and edged through the door into the corridor.

The place seemed so open and the darkness so concealing that Mole hung in the doorway, listening. He thought he heard the drip of water, somewhere near, and something else, something vibrating and thunderous far above. He started into the corridor, but his foot met something cold and hard.

The bolt. He stooped; pain burned across his back until he straightened again, the length of iron in his hand. It was some kind of weapon, at least. And he knew he would need a weapon.

He found both walls of the corridor, then walked, arms outstretched between them, eyes wide, for as long as he dared. Eventually he reached out in front of him, but felt nothing though it seemed to him he could see the end of the corridor, something slightly lighter beyond. Perhaps he was coming to a second passage perpendicular to the first, a passage lit by some distant, wavering lantern. By the time he reached the junction of the ways, the light was enough that he could see his hands. Pressing himself against the wall, he peered into the second corridor, toward the source of light.

At once he heard footfalls and saw not a lantern but a torch, a torch coming slowly toward him, reflecting on the stone walls. He withdrew and backed against the wall; his heart pounded in his throat. Both the sound of footsteps and the torchlight on the opposite wall grew steadily.

He could not run or hide; meeting the bearer of the torch was inevitable.

Holding his breath, Mole clenched the bolt in his hand.

While Fflad was still on the threshold between dreams and waking, he thought they were stars. Stars falling in glittering spirals, stars blazing in falling rings, stars pale and silver and wind-brushed, stars hard and cold like the edge of a winter moon. But after he rubbed his eyes, the stars became snowflakes, snowflakes drifting out of the night sky into the pallid glow of the dying campfire.

Arien, seated on a rock, was watching them. Her blanket encircled her shoulders, but her hair spilled over it, hiding her face.

"Arien?" Fflad said, sleepily. "Still up?"

She looked down at him, smiling. "I couldn't sleep."

"Dreadful weather," Fflad remarked, bringing his hands beneath his blanket. "Winter's come early."

"That's Branddabon's doing. Do you remember how Ammar made it always winter?"

"Yes. But it was never this cold."

"Maybe not. But it was cold then, too."

Fflad didn't answer. Instead, he examined Arien's face. "Something's wrong," he said. "You're worried about Mole, aren't you?"

She nodded. "Aren't *you?*"

"Yes. But Arien, you know that Mole's always been able to take care of himself. He'll be all right, I'm sure."

"I'm not sure, Fflad." Brushing her hair aside, she stared at him. "It might be my imagination, but I *feel* things about Mole. Tonight I have the feeling that he's in a lot of pain—"

Fflad grimaced. "Arien, don't do that to yourself. Worrying about Mole won't help him. At least for the time being, there's nothing we can do for him—"

"Isn't there?" Arien said, looking at him. "Isn't there? Oh, Fflad. If you only knew!"

"You can tell me," Fflad offered. "After all, we're twins."

But Arien didn't seem to hear him. She watched the snow coming down and stirred the coals back to flame with a stick. "If only the darkness weren't so frail, so thin," she muttered to herself, "and the fire beyond so fierce." She pulled her blanket around her. "Oh Fflad! Do you think I'm selfish?"

Fflad raised his eyebrows. "I don't know what you mean! You're one of the least selfish people I know."

She bowed her head. "I was afraid you'd say that."

"Go to sleep, Arien," Fflad whispered. "Morning isn't very far off."

She gave him a pale smile. "I know," she said.

Mole heard the snapping of the torch, and he tried to shrink back into the shadows as it advanced toward him. He could see nothing of the person who held it, only fingers that curled around it. Perhaps it was the hand, a small, pale one rather than a thick, hairy one, that kept Mole from springing at whoever held it.

Instead he hesitated in the shadows. He crouched down as

the torch swung into view and kept the bolt ready in his hand.

The torch stopped. Then, with a gasp from the person behind it, it fell. In the same instant, Mole burst from the shadows and caught it up. Brandishing it in one hand and the bolt in the other, he forced the torchbearer against the wall.

A squeal of fear and surprise. "Mole! Mole! What are you doing?"

Mole brought the torch down. "Mair?" he questioned, growing limp. "Mair! I thought you were a goblin or one of Branddabon's henchmen. What on earth are you doing down here?"

"Trying to find you. Mole, you look dreadful. What have they done to you?"

"It doesn't matter," he said. "I'm all right."

Taking the torch from him, Mair reached out and touched one of the weals on his shoulder. Both of them winced. "Come on," she said. "I'm taking you out of here."

"How did you know I was here? What's going on? Has Branddabon declared himself? Or have the kings come already?"

"You're babbling," Mair said. "Come on. I'll answer your questions later. Right now we've got to leave. That creature that lives down here will be back any minute."

They started to follow the passage by the light of Mair's torch. Mole found himself limping, hardly able to keep up with her. When she saw him, she crooked her arm in his and pulled him along.

"Where's your father?" Mole asked her.

"At the wall," she said, her face expressionless. "An army has crossed the Thrine in the storm. They'll go to battle within an hour."

"An army? What army? Have the Kings come?"

"I don't know," Mair said. "All I know is that the High King says they're enemies, traitors. All I know is that they're going to attack the walls. The High King says—"

"There is no High King," Mole said. "He's dead! The man who's pretending to be the High King is a sorcerer, an evil sorcerer named Branddabon—"

"I've heard such rumors," Mair said, "but my father says they aren't true. He says that the High King has gone mad, but we must defend him against his enemies anyway. That's the high law. Hurry, Mole."

They started up a narrow flight of steps. "Would the High King, even a mad High King, have done *this* to me?" Mole was breathing hard. "Look at me, Mair. Look at me! Would the High King have let this happen to me?"

Mair halted. "Does it matter, Mole?" she said fiercely. "Does it matter now?" Her eyes glinted in the torchlight. "The world is falling to pieces. Does it matter whether the High King's a sorcerer or whether he's mad?"

"Yes," Mole said, "yes, it does. Because if he's a sorcerer, he'll find the Book of Gath and then the world really will fall to pieces!"

"Mole," she said, "you're delirious!"

He seized her arm. "Mair, I've never thought more clearly in my life. Mair, look at me. You've come this far to help me. I need you to help me more, to help me find the Sword and stop this thing from happening. Trust me, Mair."

She looked at the floor. Then, slowly, she nodded.

"Where's Bran—I mean, where's the High King?"

"I don't know." She sniffed. "I don't have any idea. All I know is that most of them—the men who guard the Royal Quarters and all these dungeons—went to the walls. That's why I came; I wanted to come sooner, Mole. I knew they had you here. Gwenith saw them taking you here weeks ago, in the middle of the night. But Mole, I couldn't make myself come before. I'm not brave like Arien."

Mole gave her a slight smile. "You have, perhaps, more courage than you know."

"I came to help you," Mair said, her lip trembling. "And I will. I'll find new clothes for you, food and drink. I'll keep you hidden someplace, someplace where they'll never find you. And I won't tell them where you are, even if they try to torture me."

"Mair, that's not the kind of help I need. Not right now. The kind of help I *really* need you can't give—" He hesitated, then brightened. "Or can you? Mair, weren't you a lady-in-waiting once?"

She started to pull him up the stairs. "Yes," she said, "but that was a long time ago, when I was a little girl, before Princess Geniolien went to Crywyll to study. But Mole, what does that matter—"

"I said you'd have to trust me—"

"All right, but keep going. We're almost out now." A faint light, like sunlight through dust or twilight, drifted down on the stairs.

"Ladies-in-waiting run errands for the royal family," Mole said, shuddering in the sudden drafts of freezing air. "Do you remember some of the places the High King put things for safekeeping?"

"There were dozens," Mair said, "too many to remember." She dropped the torch into a bucket on the top stair. The stairway ended at an iron-bar door, fastened with a lock. Beyond it snowflakes danced to obscure the garden Mole remembered as the one beneath Gion's balcony.

"Name some of them," Mole prompted.

Mair peered out in the snow with a worried frown. "This place was one," she said. "It was never meant to be a dungeon, only a storehouse for treasure and food."

"What were some of the others?"

Mair drew a ring of large keys from her belt. "My father's," she explained, thrusting one of them into the lock.

"What were some of the others?" Mole repeated.

As soon as the gate opened, Mair turned to him. "How do you expect me to remember at a time like this? There were dozens, I'd say, in different closets and chambers and towers. The High Princess herself had two locked rooms full of tapestries. Here, Mole, take my cloak or you'll freeze to death when we get outside."

Mole took the cloak from Mair. He frowned. "No, Branddabon will have searched all the obvious places. Did you ever hear about anywhere secret, anywhere out of the ordinary?"

Before she answered, Mair helped Mole draw the cloak around him. He flinched when it rested on his back, and her face reflected the pain in his. "I can't remember anyplace like that."

"You've got to," Mole prodded her. "Try. Think."

But Mair looked away into the snow. Shapes of trees reared up in the distance. "We can't stay here, Mole. The guards won't be away for long. They'll be back, maybe sooner than we think."

"If a battle is about to start," Mole said, "they won't be back at all. I think I hear war horns now. None of that's important, Mair. The only thing that's important is for you to remember."

"A secret hiding place?"

"Yes. Think."

Mair closed her eyes, but she soon opened them. "I'm trying, Mole, but I can't remember. Maybe there's nothing for me to remember. Because every time the High King or any of the lords had something secret to talk about or to hide, they shut themselves up away from everybody else, in the hall of thrones."

Mole gripped her arms. "The hall of thrones?"

"Yes," Mair said, chewing her lip. "They would stay in there for hours sometimes. I remember spying on them through the windows when I was little. It was all so mysterious to me then. Once, Princess Geniolien took her golden medallion and never brought it back out again."

"The hall of thrones," Mole murmured. "That's it!"

"What do you mean?"

"It's the place Gion hid the Sword. I'm almost sure of it. Branddabon's searched the whole castle, but he couldn't search a secret hiding place only the royal family knew about—"

"Neither can you," Mair returned. "Even if your Sword is in the hall of thrones, how will you find it? Especially, how will you be able to look for it without getting caught?"

"I've got to look for it. I've got to find it. If Branddabon wants it so badly, he must be afraid of it. And as far as the danger of looking for it is concerned, no one will be in the hall of thrones. Not during a battle. I'd be at least as safe there as I am here."

Mair stared at him. "You're going to the hall of thrones!"

"Yes," Mole said. "Now. I can't afford to wait."

"Shouldn't you eat something first? What good will it do to find the Sword if you faint from hunger right afterward?"

"No time," Mole said, pushing through the gate into the snow.

"Then take me with you. Let me help you search."

Mole stopped. He put his hand on Mair's shoulder. "You've put yourself in enough danger for me already," he said. "And one has the same chance of finding the secret place in the hall of thrones as two. And one person has a better chance of getting there without being discovered. No, Mair, go back to your room. Lock the door. If I can't find anything in the hall of thrones, if I need your help, I'll come to you. I'll knock on your door three times, pause, then knock three times again, so you'll know it's me. Do you understand?"

Slowly Mair nodded. Flakes of snow dotted her dark hair as, after a final look at Mole, she turned away and disappeared into the snowstorm.

After pausing to gain his bearings, Mole hurried from the courtyard on a path he knew led directly to the hall of thrones. He knew of longer, less traveled ways, but he didn't want to waste time, and he knew that the falling snow would help conceal him. He caught a handful of water from an ice-crusted fountain to ease his thirst, and kept his hunger and weakness at bay with fear, a cold fear that grew with the rumbling noise Mole began to detect from far away. Only when the shrill of distant war horns punctuated the roar did he remember that the armies of the kings were attacking the wall. He had to help them. He had to find the Sword.

Though Mair's cloak shielded him from the snow, it didn't keep his bare feet from the ice, and soon, because his toes were numb, he tripped, sprawling onto the walk. Shocked and shivering, he scrambled up and limped along, cradling scraped arms inside his cloak. But he used his reawakened pain to sharpen his mind and eyes; when he saw a blur ahead, he slipped behind a thornbush until the danger, two guards hurrying toward the walls, passed him.

Finally he reached the steps of the hall of thrones. He lingered there long enough to peer over the common toward the east wall, from which he heard a crackling sound over the shouts of warriors. He saw a sheet of flame shoot up near the east gate, then sink back beneath the wall. *Fire powder,* Mole thought, unbelieving. Yet it couldn't be, for the wall where the flames had risen seemed unshaken.

The Sword, his mind growled, *find the Sword.*

He tried the doors, but they were locked. He wished he'd asked Mair for her father's keys until he realized that the hall doors, like the one in his prison, were barred, not locked. Bringing the iron bolt from his cloak pocket, he tried to release the inside bar the same way he had removed the bolt of his prison, but the crack in the doors was too narrow.

He looked upward. The peak of the roof loomed above him. Beneath it were columns of stone interspersed with high windows. He could not hope to break through the stone or climb to the windows. But there was another door to the hall, he remembered, a small door that led in from the kitchens at its back.

Backtracking along the side of the hall, Mole found the door to the kitchen open; a dust of snow swept across the threshold. Inside it was dark and cold. The air tasted of snow and smelled of frozen cooking fat. Mole glimpsed a cauldron from which beardlike icicles hung and a broom near the door that was mottled with snow. He edged along in the darkness until he came to a door; he opened it, but found only burlap sacks of flour. He groped further, found another door and opened it.

Dust-laden sunlight met him, making him sneeze. He was looking through a low doorway into the great vault of the hall. He could scarcely see the main doors at the far end because of the dust, which, drifting through pale light from snow-dimmed windows, swam in the hall like a snowstorm itself. Suddenly tense, Mole moved into the hall and shut the door behind him.

The hall of thrones was colder than the air outside. Perhaps it was because of the ice-colored stone beneath the cavern-shaped dome. Perhaps it was the frozen ground beneath the long, dust-faded carpets and the marble floors. Perhaps it was a hidden draft, a frosty breath that made the tapestries swing back and forth slightly. Mole had felt such cold once before, but he couldn't remember where. He only recalled that such cold had to do with fear, unexplained fear.

He swallowed, clasped the throat of his cloak with his hand, then started to follow the wall away from the thrones, running his free hand along the flawless stone-work beneath the tapestries.

· 11 ·

Gifts of Parting

KING ELLARWY, BEARD crusted with snow, waited for the last troop of Thrinedor warriors to cross the river. He sat astride a horse whose head was bent into the wind; the wind howled across the river ice, hissed in the empty trees, and moaned in the horse's trappings. Shielding their eyes against the snow, Berrian and Ellari stood beside their father. In a brake of aspens nearby, Fflad held the reins of three more horses, and in the shelter of the trees, Geniolien, Merani, and Arien were almost lost in a mist of snow.

King Ellarwy's face softened when the last rider urged his horse up the near bank. "We're lucky to get across the ice here," he said. "The ice swallowed a Crywyll company farther up river."

"We're already at battle," Berrian said grimly. "The sorcerer is throwing the full power of his magic at us!"

Ellari shivered in agreement as King Ellarwy turned his horse to follow along the river. But the king saw the girls huddled in the trees and wheeled his horse toward them. "Remember, all of you," he said to them, "you're not to go anywhere near the battle. Especially you, Merani, so don't frown like that. I want you to protect the others with that bow of yours. Stay here; build a fire if you can. We'll be back as soon as the battle's over."

King Ellarwy shouted to his sons. "Mount up, the rest of you. Come on, or we'll miss the battle altogether."

"One moment," Fflad said. Leaving the reins to Ellari, he went to Arien and took both her hands in his. "I want you to watch out for goblins," he said, "this forest may be full of them."

"I think," Arien replied, "that all the goblins have gathered at Ranath Drallm or are deep in their lairs to weather the storm. You're the one who should be careful. You are, after all, a poet, not a warrior. And besides, you're the only real brother I've ever had, so I want you to take care of yourself."

"You're my only sister," Fflad said, looking down, "real or otherwise. And I'll come back to you, if I can, when the battle's done. But I won't take care of myself. That's not a rule of war."

Smiling at him, she slowly nodded. Then as he mounted his horse, she said, "If you get into Ranath Drallm, find Mole for me. And make sure he's well before you come back to me."

"I will," Fflad said. "You know I will."

Meanwhile, Ellari went to Merani, reaching into his cloak as he looked at her. She reddened and curled her fingers under her bow strap, but she smiled when Ellari said her name. "Merani, I don't know exactly what to say, but I would like to give you this, to keep safe, just in case something happens to me in the battle—"

"Nothing will happen to you," Merani said. "It can't."

Ellari pressed his lips. "Anyway, I want you to have this." He brought out the silver drinking flask he had found in the goblin lair. Solemnly he handed it to Merani.

"Thank you," she said. She looked away, but said, hugging the flask against her, "Be careful, Ellari."

"In the middle of all these farewells," Berrian said to Geniolien from astride his horse, "it seems that you and I are left as a pair. I hope to see you again, though I dreamed last night that I never saw you crowned High Queen."

"Does that mean, Prince Berrian," Geniolien replied, "that you missed my coronation or that I am never to be crowned at all?"

"It means," Berrian said, "that I didn't sleep well last night and that I had strange dreams." His face went pale, even against the snow. "I don't know why I dreamed of snow and fire and death, for my parting here is less bitter than it is for the rest of you. All of you are saying farewell to each other, but I'm going to Drallm to where Gwenith is waiting for me to deliver her—"

"Much more talk," King Ellarwy said, "and we won't be able to catch up with the rest of the army. Come on, Berrian. Ellari. Fflad."

"Farewell," Geniolien called out, "and good luck!"

Berrian waved to them as the horses started away. "Goodbye," he said.

As soon as they disappeared into the snow, Merani took stock of her surroundings. If she was to defend Arien and Geniolien, she ought to anticipate how danger might come on them. After fastening Ellari's flask to her belt, she looked across the blue ice of the Thrine toward the squat, naked hills blurred by the storm. In the open ground between the riverbanks, the wind had already blasted away the prints of men and horses.

A note from King Ellarwy's battle horn, muted by the wind, cried out in the snow-hidden distance.

"I wish they'd left us horses." Shivering, Merani faced Geniolien.

"I don't think we'll need them," Geniolien said. "If we win the battle, King Ellarwy will come back for us. If we don't—"

"If they don't," Arien finished, "running won't do any good."

"Why not?" Merani demanded. "My bow and a couple of horses could get us to Taranil, or even to Ranath Thrine."

"If the kings are defeated," Arien said, "darkness will come. The sorcerer will be able to conquer the other strongholds of the kingdoms at his leisure. Or he might send out an enchanted winter, as Ammar did. Or, worse, he might find what is hidden in the vaults of Drallm, the Book of Gath, with which he can bring utter darkness—"

Geniolien's lip curled. "Let's find some shelter, at least," she said.

They moved deeper into the trees. Beneath the pines, the wind's moan was fainter, and the loose snow more shallow. But it was still cold.

Geniolien rubbed her hands together under her mantle. "If we can manage it," she said, "we ought to build a fire."

While Arien and Geniolien gathered wood, Merani found the tinder box in her pack. The wood, however, was frozen and ice-crusted, and only after several attempts did Merani nurse to life a wobbly orange flame. "You're an enchantress,

Merani," Arien said when the blaze crackled and danced over the wood.

"Not exactly," Merani said, cheeks ruddy from the heat of the fire. "I lived in the wilds of Fellheath, that's all."

They all pressed close to the flames. As the fire grew, Merani watched the snow on her hood slush, then drop away. But her worry did not disappear. She listened for the winding of horns, but she heard only the voice of the flames.

"It's hard to say good-bye," Arien said at length.

"I know what you mean," Geniolien said. "I haven't said good-bye to Gion yet. Not really."

"I never said good-bye to my father," Merani said. "And I never will."

Arien smiled faintly. "Sometimes you have to say good-bye," she said. "And I think that after this battle, all of us will have some good-byes to make."

The conversation drifted away into an uncomfortable silence punctuated by the sounds of snow and flames. Whenever an ember snapped, Merani tensed. She heard other sounds, too: peeps from Cwyller sheltered in her cloak, distant groans that might have been wind, the rattle of unknown things in the river reeds, and the hum of wingbeats high in the clouds.

"I wish—" Merani said suddenly.

"Don't wish," Geniolien said. "Wishes only cause problems. I don't know if any evil will come of my wish that strengthens Drallm's walls, but it can't be helpful to have the binding spell *against* us instead of *for* us."

"I wish," Merani repeated, "that we could see how the battle is going. I ought to be there instead of here. King Ellarwy has many good warriors, but he doesn't have any good archers—"

"Yes," Geniolien said, "it would be nice to see what's happening."

"Maybe," Arien said, staring at Merani, "there is a way, a way to see Mole and Berrian and Fflad. That flask Ellari gave you—where did he get it?"

"In a goblin lair. But it isn't of goblin make; it's older. It's a treasure." Merani folded her hands around the flask.

"Hand it to me, would you?"

"But Ellari gave it to me for safekeeping." Merani frowned at Arien. "I shouldn't just pass it around."

"Please, Merani. I'll be careful. It's just that I noticed—"

Merani cradled the flask in her arms.

"Merani! Do you want to see the battle or don't you?"

Hesitating, Merani unfastened the flask from her belt and handed it to Arien, who turned it in the firelight.

"Be careful," Merani cried out, "or you'll drop it in the fire!"

Arien put the flask in her lap and unscrewed the cap. "This was made in Fellheath," she said. "One of King Daerwyn's men had one like it. When we were at Rathvidrian after the battle, he showed me what it was and what power it had. Such things used to belong to wizards. Whether the wizard ended up in the same goblin lair as his flask, I don't know. But unless I'm mistaken, we may be able to see something of the battle."

"How?" Geniolien asked.

Arien extended her arm over a patch of ground that was free from snow. She poured water from the flask, enough to make a pool the size of a pane of glass. The puddle quickly froze to ice.

Merani snatched the flask back, then crouched near the ice for a better look. The frozen surface of the pool, milky and glass-smooth, mirrored the snowflakes falling on its edges. Above, it showed the leaden sky and the boughs of winter pine.

"I don't see anything," Merani said.

"Maybe your flask isn't magical, after all," Arien said. "I could be mistaken. But if the flask had belonged to a Fellheath wizard, you would have been able to see what you most wanted to in the water."

"I don't see anything but snowflakes," Geniolien said.

"Those aren't snowflakes," Merani contradicted. She peered into the mirror. "Those are warriors on a snowy hill!"

"So they are," Geniolien exclaimed. "And that's the east wall, covered with defenders, black with smoke. People are putting things up against the wall, then running back. What is it? I see fire—"

"Goblin fire powder!" Merani said, pushing for a better view of the ice. "King Daerwyn must have brought it from Fellheath. The goblins they captured had a lot, I think."

"How awful!" Geniolien said. "Look! It isn't doing any good. But, then, how could it?" Geniolien, chalk pale, looked at Merani. "My wish has done more damage than I'd thought. Merani, they've based their whole battle plan on making a gap in the wall with fire powder. But they can't. They're being driven back by the archers."

"The archers of Drallm," Merani said dully, "are deadly."

"What? Are they trying to go for the walls again?" Geniolien's fists cut off Merani's view. "Oh, Arien. I can't see clearly. Can you tell me what's happening now?"

"No," Arien said. "Because I'm not seeing what you're seeing. I'm seeing something else besides the battle, something I don't understand at all. It's a quiet, stony place—"

"Look!" Merani burst out. "Look what's happening now!"

"I think they've realized the fire powder won't work," Geniolien said. "They're falling back. But they're falling back too quickly. That rain of arrows from the walls is taking a toll!"

"What are they doing now?" Merani said. "Some of them have gone into the forest near the north wall. They're coming out again. They're carrying something. It's a log—no, a tree trunk. It's a ram. Yes, it's a ram!"

"But what will they do with it? Surely they don't plan to break down the gate! The gates are all too well fortified. They'd lose too many men bringing that ram to the gate. But they are! Look! The men by the river are dismounting, coming to help carry the ram. I see that young captain, Eheran, I think his name is. Wait! What's going on now? I could understand so much better if I could hear!"

"Maybe you could if you didn't talk so much," Arien said. "And move back, please. I can't be sure, but I think I see . . ." Arien didn't finish.

Merani, meanwhile, had grown enough accustomed to the mirror to understand the formation of the battle. She could see that the men of Thrinedor and Vivrandon were forming a wedge around the ram; they were being harassed at their flanks by enemy horsemen. Most of the castle guard, however, had gathered on the wall above the gate, where archers rained arrows on the approaching ram. Many men had fallen already; the ram left bodies in its wake that the snow began to cover.

"The ram's slowing down," Merani said.

"By the Emperor," Geniolien said. "I see men I know on both sides. On the walls are Enetoth and Evetoth, my brother's senior captains. And there's Lord Morin! And dear old Lord Melidor. How awful! Please, don't kill one another!" As if the moving figures on the ice could hear her, Geniolien shouted to them.

"I can see the kings' men, too," Merani said. "I can see Gwael the Bard, and Fflad, and Prince Gareth. I wonder where

Ellari is—there? Yes, that's him. He doesn't have a horse!"

The ram, wobbly and staggering, slowed its advance toward the gate. Arrows flew from the wall. Around the ram a sea of battle swelled. King Ellarwy and King Daerwyn were trying to rally the kings' horsemen around three tattered banners.

"The ram!" Geniolien moaned. "The ram! It's stopped!"

"It's going backwards!" Merani said. "Someone *do* something!"

"Someone is," Geniolien returned. "Look, Merani. Can you see that sword flash? Someone has broken off from the ram. He's throwing himself against that troop of castle horsemen. I can't tell who it is, but he doesn't look very old. By the Emperor, it's Berrian! Prince Berrian!"

"He's doing wonders," Merani said, smiling for the first time. "Look at the horsemen fall back. They're afraid of him!"

"But look! He's hurt. He's holding his shoulder!"

"But he's going back to the ram. He's waving for the others to join him. He's lifting the ram." Merani bit her fist. "Ellari's there."

"Berrian!" Geniolien shouted. "Berrian's got the ram moving again!"

"The archers are shooting at him, though," Merani said. "But the ram's getting near the gate. Oh! Berrian's hit!"

"Yes," Geniolien said. "But he isn't stopping."

"I see blood," Merani said in a lower voice. "Another arrow's hit him!"

"And another!" Geniolien said. "I can't bear to watch."

"I can't help but watch," Merani said. But she cringed as she saw Berrian stagger. She glimpsed his face, taut and pale, but shining with determination.

Then the ram met the gate. Both shuddered. The ram fell back, but then swing forward again.

It struck again. Neither Merani nor Geniolien spoke. Merani saw sweat mingled with blood on Berrian's face.

Again the ram struck. Geniolien leaped to her feet. "The gate's down! It's broken! I saw it crash. It's down!"

"But so is Berrian!" Merani wailed. "I saw him fall. They must be rushing right over him trying to get in the gate."

Geniolien looked away from the mirror. "Berrian won't be able to come to my coronation," she said softly, looking at the river. "He knew it."

Merani looked to Arien then, and found her far more upset

than she expected. Arien's fingers shook against her cheeks, her eyes were fixed on the mirror, and a single tear dropped into the fire, hissing strangely in the flames. At the same time the fire seemed to burn in Arien's eyes like fury. And it seemed to Merani, although she was still too shocked by Berrian's death to think clearly, that Arien could neither hear nor see, that she was caught on a brink between blinding forces of fire and ice.

Merani followed Arien's stare to the mirror, but she saw only a pool of cracked ice, dull like the sky, that fast was being covered with snow. Merani looked up again.

But she saw only the rush of snow over the far hills, and nearer, the drifting of snow across an empty log.

Arien had vanished.

The last curve of stonework ended at the kitchen door. Mole found himself in the same place he had begun his search. And nothing had changed; he still had found no clue to the location of the Sword, and the urgency he had sensed earlier, if anything, had increased.

His sense of apprehension centered, it seemed, on the great throne; he had found himself glancing at it all during his search. From the back, the throne was almost lost in shadow; Mole could make out only a few markings, chips of stone, on its back.

Markings.

He froze, squinting, took a step nearer. On the lower half of the throne, the markings seemed almost to create a square just smaller than the edge of the stone. When he came closer, he saw that the markings were grooves that some stoneworker had done his best to conceal.

Kneeling quickly, Mole pushed the tips of his fingers into either side of the square. He pulled, but nothing happened. If this was the vault he was looking for, he realized, there was a good chance it was sealed by magic. All the same, it seemed that if he could just dig his fingers deep enough in the cracks, he could lift out the back of the throne. He tried again, pushing inward until his hands ached. Then, lifting and thrusting against the throne with his feet, Mole pulled a window-sized plate of stone into his lap.

He peered into the hollow under the seat of the throne, but he saw nothing. Reaching in, he touched something that was certainly a gem; but to his disappointment, it belonged to a bracelet, not his Sword. He stretched his arm more deeply in to find that the hollow went far beneath the throne. Groping, he felt cold metal, first a crown, next another bracelet, and last something heavy and jewel-crusted, something he could see glinting slightly as he dragged it out of the throne. The Sword.

Mole cried out when the half light of the hall lit the Sword's sapphires.

"Quiet, now," urged the voice of the Sword. "You may not be alone here."

"That doesn't matter anymore," Mole returned. Throwing back his cloak, Mole buckled the swordbelt on his waist, tested the hilt in his grip, then, sheathing the Sword, he hurriedly replaced the plate of rock over the back of the throne.

The sounds of battle, before distant and remote, seemed to be coming from just outside the hall. Mole thought he heard Captain Paladain's war horn and King Ellarwy's voice. He ran from behind the thrones, bound for the great doors.

But in front of the great throne he froze. His skin prickled. Something like a damp shadow closed over him. He spun around.

A man Mole had never seen before sat in the high throne. He wore a cloak and a hood that seemed to be webbed of shadows; the cloak covered the man's feet and all of his arms except for grey hands, like cobweb-covered claws. One hand was missing a finger, and on the same finger of the opposite hand rested an iron ring stamped with a strange and twisted device. The man's face, what Mole could glimpse of it in the shadow of the hood, looked like that of a man dead several days, for the flesh around the narrow lips was spotted and grey. The eyes seemed to sparkle, more precisely they seemed to glow, yellow-green, from the depths of the hood.

Mole felt himself shudder and snatch for the Sword. "Brand-dabon!" he said.

The ringed finger twitched slightly. "I can recognize you, too, now," the sorcerer said. "That Sword makes it easier, you know."

"You've been here all the time, in that throne!" Mole burst out, backing away. "I couldn't see you, but I *felt* you."

The sorcerer laughed. "You were so eager. So eager to find that Sword. And just as I thought, you knew more about the Sword than you told Maglaw's whip."

Mole drew the Sword and thrust it out toward Branddabon. It glinted coldly in the snowy light from the windows. "You'll die, Branddabon," Mole said. "Just like Ammar and the Black Counselor, you'll die."

"No, I won't," Branddabon said, coolly. Though Mole took a step toward him, he did not move. "For one thing, I'm wiser than any other sorcerer yet to come to the North. I'm prepared for both you and your Sword. You'll never get near me. You're the one who will die, even though your friends have broken the gate and are on their way here." The sorcerer's eyes glittered. "They will all die. All of them. Because I have this."

One of the claw hands lifted, palm up, toward the light. What Mole had thought to be a ring darkened, swelled, grew until it hid all of the sorcerer's hand. And Mole realized, by the horror he felt and by the sudden smell of rottenness, that Branddabon held a book. The Book of Gath.

Grinning, the sorcerer lifted his other hand. It seemed to grow longer, extending over the floor toward Mole. Mole tried to back away, but he fell. The Sword clattered to the flagstones, where a tendril of shadow wrapped around it to drag it slowly toward the great throne. Mole dived and caught the Sword's hilt, but pain split his body. The hilt scorched his hand; he felt dark flames burning between his fingers. But he didn't let go, not even when a second shadow blow hit him.

Then a force, like a freezing wind, pierced his skull. Crying out, Mole released the Sword, then threw his hands to his ears. But the pain in his head did not stop, and he saw the Sword slide away across the floor, toward the grimacing creature on the high throne.

"Emperor!" he cried. "Emperor, help me!"

At once a searing flash filled the hall of thrones. A dozen torches along the walls sprang to life. A web of fire flickered in the heights of the ceiling, glowing against the high windows. The pain in Mole's head snapped away, and looking up, he saw the sorcerer, flame-lit, gaping at something across the room. Turning around, Mole saw a burst of light that filled the far end of the hall fringed with golden flames whose tongues licked away the last shadows near the great throne. In the center of the glow, garbed in fire, arms outstretched, was Arien.

Mole tried to call to her, but a wave of darkness pushed him down, smothering him, freezing him. He heard voices of imps chattering in his ears. A moment later light washed over him again, and he saw the sorcerer, thrown again at bay, raising the Book.

"Quickly!" Arien's voice boomed against the advancing darkness. "Quickly, Mole! My power can't hold him for long! He's got the Book! Kill him, Mole! Kill him!"

Staggering up, Mole snatched the Sword. Darkness hung like a mist around Branddabon, growing, billowing outward. Mole fancied he heard Arien moan. The sorcerer's eyes flashed. "Think before you try to kill me," Branddabon sneered. "Think! Kill me, and I give you this curse and this promise: you will have an unhappy life, and Arien, who now protects you, will be lost to you forever!"

Mole halted; he pulled the Sword back. Visions of Arien raced through his mind.

But, clasping both hands firmly on the hilt of the Sword, he threw himself against the sorcerer, thrusting the Sword downward through the frozen fabric of the Book, into the cloaked shadow beyond.

Thunder, unless it was Branddabon's scream, split Mole's ears. The hall of thrones shook. Shadows whirled and burst in towers of flame; fire much hotter than Arien's blinded him. Letting go of the Sword, Mole fell back. He saw the Sword and the Book combine into a single entity of sparks and shadow, the Book engulfing, quenching, the Sword searing, blazing. Lightning struck upward. Another fountain of fire shot up, hissing against the high arches, catching onto tapestries that plummeted down in billowing flames.

Lying on his side, only half-conscious, Mole watched the white blaze shrink away to a crackling yellow, then to a dull saffron, then to a quiet ruby in the darkness. Feeling empty, he laid his head back; he heard the winds against the high windows hiss and die.

· 12 ·

Song

THE DEEP WINTER night was pricked with ivory stars. Snow, untouched by wind, lay on the castle hill. The sea beat against the rocks and washed against the moonlit water of the Thrine.

Among the willows by the sea, a mound had been raised. There, a hundred and eighty-three torches glowed on a throng that had assembled to honor the fallen of the Battle of the East Gate.

Near the hill, in shadow, King Ellarwy, Lord Morin, and King Daerwyn stood. In front of them Gwael the Bard knelt, plucking notes from a golden harp and singing in a low voice:

> "Beneath bare branches shadows grow
> To cast on earth a silent snow.
> But though the light drains from the west,
> Blossoms bloom where good men rest.
>
> Winter's icicles, like rust,
> Grind the ground to solemn dust.
> But spring will come though winter weep,
> And blossoms bloom where good men sleep."

"Isn't it beautiful?" Fflad said to Mole as they stood together watching. "I couldn't have made up a better lament myself."

155

"It is lovely," Arien said, tugging her cloak more tightly around her, "but sad."

Mole said nothing.

"Come on," Fflad said, nudging Mole, "cheer up. We've lost friends on both sides, but things will be better now. The sorcerer is dead. And the Book is destroyed."

"And so is the Sword," Mole said.

"Its task was finished," Arien said. "It was destined to be lost when the last of the three sorcerers was killed, when that last ruby on the hilt became a sapphire."

"I'll miss it all the same," Mole said. "But I'll miss other things more. I'll miss Berrian most of all—"

Arien looked at the torches. "Don't you see, Mole?" she said. "Just like the Sword—Paladain, Fendwr, Berrian, and all the others—their task was complete."

Mole paused, then said, "He died well. Like a prince."

"And he won the battle for us." Fflad sighed.

Arien frowned. "He and Mole."

Silence followed.

"Tomorrow night will be a more cheerful one, I think," Fflad said. "The council will help us forget some of the awful things that have happened. And it will be interesting to see who they choose to take High King Gion's crown."

"And prophecies will be fulfilled," Arien said, gazing at the stars over the sea. "Many prophecies," she murmured.

• 13 •

The High Queen's Council

MOLE WAS SURPRISED to see how well the craftsmen had re-
paired the hall of thrones. The fire-blackened walls and roof
had all been sanded white again, except for one pitlike blur of
black near the great throne, most of which had been covered
with carpet. New tapestries, less dusty than the former, hung
between the windows. Torches blazed and candles flickered.
The whole hall was well-lit and completely full; people sat at
tables near the dais, on benches under the vault, on kegs and
chairs and boxes behind the colonnades. People leaned against
the pillars and piled up against the doors. Younger children sat
on their parents' laps and older children on tables. Two archers
had climbed to the dark windowsills to get a better view. Mole
had been lucky to find seats for himself and Arien near the
front of the hall; even some princes had not been allowed to
sit so near the thrones.

Yet, in spite of the cheerful atmosphere around him, Mole
was troubled. He could not forget what had happened in this
same hall. Flashes of pain returned when he looked at the
torches, and the sorcerer's last words seemed to repeat themselves in the murmur of the crowd. Arien, seated at his side,
did not seem well either. Her lips were drawn into a frown,
and when she looked at him, her eyes flickered. He took her
hand and smiled at her. She tried to smile back, but her face
twisted suddenly, and she looked away.

Holding his tongue, Mole looked toward the thrones. Only

157

four of them were filled, two on each side of the great throne. To the right, King Ellarwy of Thrinedor and King Daerwyn of Vivrandon represented the Greater Kingdoms. The third great throne, the throne of Pesten, was empty; Mole knew it had been empty for years, since the last king of Pesten, High King Eithodd's brother Llaran, had died in the goblin destruction of Ranath Caeodd. King Redwen of Crywyll and King Cashma of Sharicom were speaking from neighbor seats to the left of the great throne. The seat of the other Lesser Kingdom, Aelenwaith, was empty. Mole tried to imagine how King Eiddew would look in it. The high throne, of course, was vacant as well; to fill it was the purpose of the kings' council.

King Ellarwy, who had been chosen to conduct the meeting, stood up. When he began to speak, the crowd quieted so that his voice, though not loud, could be heard throughout the hall.

The king began by welcoming all who had come and by explaining (in too much detail, Mole thought) the purpose of the council, which everyone knew already. When all the formalities were finished, King Ellarwy sat back in his throne, and the real council began.

"I think we ought to begin," King Redwen said, "by listing all the possible candidates for the throne."

"High Princess Geniolien is Gion's declared heir," King Cashma said. "We know that already."

"Yes, but the fact that Gion died unexpectedly makes the question more complicated. He had been calling Geniolien his heir for years, but only because she was his only living relative. And while he was still alive, there was always the chance that he would marry and have a son to succeed him on the throne."

Mole looked at Princess Geniolien, who sat on the front row of benches. She seemed both beautiful and composed, but Mole saw her jaw tighten and her eyes narrow as King Redwen spoke.

"Who else," King Ellarwy asked him, "do you consider a possibility?"

"You, sir, for one," Redwen replied, "and all your sons. You're the only royal family left who has any of the blood of Llarandil, distant though it may be. Perhaps *you* should become High King."

"*I?*" King Ellarwy almost bellowed. "That's ridiculous! I completely withdraw myself from consideration. And my sons, too. Certainly we have the blood of Llarandil in us, but it's thinned by Thrine water now. Myself, I'm only fit for orchards and foggy mornings, not pomp, ceremony, and war. I hate to think what kind of High King I would make." King Ellarwy tugged at his beard, frowning at King Redwen. "And you can't claim one of my sons, either. Now that Berrian's gone, I have only seven. And I won't lose another crown prince. If there were none of the high family left, I might see things in a different light, but as long as Geniolien is here, I'm quite out of the question."

"I don't see who else is *in* question," King Daerwyn broke in. "Since Geniolien is both the declared heir and the last member of the royal family, who else could we choose? We ought to crown her High Queen at once." King Daerwyn went on to list Princess Geniolien's virtues, until Geniolien herself began to blush and whisper to Merani, who sat beside her.

A few of the observers, including Mole, clapped when Daerwyn finished.

"I've never questioned Princess Geniolien's good qualities," King Redwen said when the hall had quieted down again. "As you all know, she spent several pleasant years in my kingdom." King Redwen glanced at his son, who sat two rows behind Geniolien. "But since the battle at the east gate, I've had a chance to visit the Library of the Bards. I looked through all the old chronicles of Llarandil, and I found this." He held up a leather-bound book for all to see. "Here I found written, by Llarandil's own hand, that only a *man* will wear the high crown."

An angry murmur spread through the hall.

Prince Ellari, who sat between Geniolien and Merani, jumped to his feet. "Are you questioning the heir of the late High King?"

"No," King Redwen said coolly. "As I've said, I personally know the princess to be every good thing King Daerwyn said her to be. But the law exists, written by Llarandil himself. I can't change that."

An uncomfortable silence followed. Mole felt a hollowness in his stomach.

King Ellarwy, fingers thumping on the arm of his throne, glowered first at Ellari, then at King Redwen. "I'll thank my son to keep his thoughts to himself, at least until he inherits my throne and can speak as a king. And you, Redwen," he continued icily, "I'd like to know what you suggest we do about the high law."

King Redwen grinned. "I wouldn't be fool enough to ask that we give the throne to one not of Llarandil's blood, for the high law demands that, too. I am merely pointing out that it may be necessary to marry the princess to . . . shall we say, a man of influence who will keep the throne for her."

"Your son?" King Cashma said tautly.

King Redwen shrugged. "As one possibility."

Shouts of protest rang out from the back of the hall.

Lifting his hand for order, King Daerwyn sat forward in his throne. "As much as I hate to say it, King Redwen is right. The High Princess must, as the last survivor of her house, be crowned High Queen, but she should also marry someone capable of holding the throne for her." Shouts continued, still from the back benches. "But to marry her to the House of Crywyll or to that of any other kingdom would give that kingdom too much power. We must decide on a husband for Geniolien who is influential but of common birth."

A pause followed, but the other kings began to nod. The shouting died down in the back of the hall.

"Very well, then," King Ellarwy said. "Who?"

Lord Morin stood up. "If I may make a suggestion, sire."

"Please," said King Ellarwy. "Speak."

"One young man I know has reminded me of a king from the very day he came to Ranath Drallm. Furthermore, he has proved himself in service to the late High King and in the wars with the sorcerers. The High King himself chose this man to become High Captain. Such a man as you want is Moleander."

Mole, who had been only half-listening, realized Lord Morin's intention too late. He leaped to his feet to protest, but his rise only made an impression on the crowd. What began as a round of bravos from some of the other captains turned into cheering in the center of the hall, then a general clamor for Mole to marry Geniolien. Only a few, Mole and the princess among them, remained silent, helpless to stop the shouting.

King Ellarwy at last restored order. "This is a council of kings," he said, glaring at the crowd. "What do the kings say?"

Each of the kings in turn rose to support Moleander. Redwen did so reluctantly, but even he could not help but mention Mole's latest achievement, the slaying of Branddabon, which in itself brought a fit of scattered applause from the members of the crowd.

"It appears," King Ellarwy said, looking at Mole and Arien,

"that the council wishes Moleander to marry the High Princess."

A roar of approval, followed by cheers of "King Mole, King Mole!" disrupted the hall until the tapestries seemed to shake with the noise. For his part, Mole sank, helpless, to his seat and buried his head in his hands, not daring to look at Arien.

He felt her hand on his shoulder. "It's all right," she whispered to him. "Mole, it's all right."

"It isn't all right," he returned. "It isn't!"

"But Mole. Let me tell you something—"

Yet King Ellarwy, winding his battle horn, interrupted her. "Now, none of us here are barbarians," he said. "We ought to give both Geniolien and Moleander a say in this. What do you say, Princess?"

The High Princess rose to her feet and cleared her throat. "I think you all should know," she said, "that Moleander may already have other plans for marriage. But," she added, looking at Mole, "I will do whatever the council decides is best."

The atmosphere in the hall became breathless. "Moleander?" King Ellarwy said.

Mole stood up. A hairpin dropped somewhere in the benches. Mole looked at the High Princess, then placed his hand gently on Arien's shoulder. "I cannot marry the princess," he said. "I cannot be High King."

The uproar would have been deafening. The crowd would have brought down the tapestries, seized the torches, rushed on Mole. King Ellarwy would have been helpless and angry, the other kings fierce with indignation. Shouts, chaos, rebukes, anger—all of it poised against Mole. But a crackle of thunder and a flash of light stopped everyone.

And in the center of the hall, near a pillar, a man appeared. He was a small man, almost a dwarf, dressed in a midnight-blue robe that was too big for him. But by no means was he comical, for his eyes flamed, and he held a stout yew staff in one hand.

Gwarthan. The name slipped from one tongue to another.

The wizard, eyebrows bristling, made his way to Mole. "I've come to straighten things out," he said briskly. "I would have been here sooner, but I was fighting a war myself, with goblins and warlocks in the Great Forest. And I'm in no mood for further quarrels." He thrust the yew staff toward the back of the hall. "Now, I happen to know what you're bickering about, and I happen to know the answer to the question you should have been asking yourselves ever since Mole killed the sorcerer Ammar. Some of you ought to have asked and figured it out for yourselves by now, just as I have; but to save time, I'll spell it all out for you."

Mole felt puzzled, but a few of the Drallm nobles, among them Lord Morin, began to nod and beam at Mole as if they were seeing him for the first time.

"I've heard lots of nonsense about laws this evening," Gwarthan went on. "Since you're so fond of laws, let me give you another one. In the kingdoms, cousins may not marry."

King Redwen objected, "What does that have to do with anything?"

"Dense!" Gwarthan exclaimed. "What I'm telling you is that Princess Geniolien and Captain Moleander are cousins—they can't marry. Surely you can see how much Moleander looks like High King Gion. There's a strong family resemblance among the descendants of Llarandil the Great!"

"What you say can't be true," Mole protested.

"Yes!" someone shouted. "That's impossible!"

"Some of you have short memories, then," Lord Morin said. "Don't any of you remember that High King Gwyram, who built this fortress, had twin sons? One, Eithodd, became High King; and the younger twin, Llaren, became both High Captain and King of Pesten. King Llaran's wife, Ysgarlad, bore a son at Ranath Caeodd before it was destroyed. And because both Llaran and Ysgarlad were killed, people thought their son was dead, too."

Wide-eyed, Mole looked at Arien. She squeezed his arm.

"The son of Llaran is not dead," Gwarthan said, watching Mole. "His mother hid him in the briars near the castle. A wise man named Rhawn found him and cared for him during the reign of Ammar, not knowing who he was. He grew up ignorant of his heritage. But he is a direct descendant of Llarandil and a cousin to the late High King."

The hall was utterly quiet.

"And just in case any of you don't believe me," Gwarthan went on, "I have proof. First, King Ellarwy, would you tell the council the two symbols of the royal House of Llarandil?"

"The sun is the first," Ellarwy replied. "It was Llarandil's own badge."

"And the second?"

King Ellarway scratched his head. "I think ... it's the ash tree, because of the strength and durability of its wood."

Gwarthan smiled. "Very good. Now, Moleander, show the council the staff you've been carrying with you, using to guide you, from the very day you left Rhawn's cave."

Slowly Mole held up the ash staff. It gleamed in the torchlight.

"There is proof, enough, I think. Fflad will not even have to bring out his binding ring. But let me tell you how *I* discovered that Mole was Llaran's missing son. The verse I'm going to recite for you was written by High Queen Cara, Llarandil's wife, who was a Daughter of Amreth. All of you, but Mole in particular, will see how her prophecy has all come true." Closing his eyes, the wizard began:

> "Son of Thorn
> Through woods has passed
> O'er tossing sea,
> Through worlds grey,
> And mountains green,
> To reign at last
> In seven seats at mouth of One
> With snow-white walls, strong and fast,
> Falling ne'er by binding spells
> Brought by her from distant vales.
>
> Gone with Goodblade
> And robe unspun,
> With Amreth's daughter,
> With him of Sharicom.
> Gone with music, lore, and wisdom.
> Parted from him who yearns to go
> Into the lands of ice and snow.
> Doomed to mourn for him who falls
> In battle at a kingdom's walls."

The words of the verse, like a half-remembered rhyme of childhood, echoed in Mole's mind. Each line brought a picture of himself or of his friends. Each line spoke of his life.

"Now, is there anyone who doubts that Moleander is the lost son of Llaran?" Gwarthan looked over the crowd, but saw no protest. Mole himself felt that he was least sure of Gwarthan's statement. "Now," Gwarthan continued, turning to the kings, "will any of you deny that Mole ought to be given the High Crown?"

King Ellarwy shook his head. "Not I. Moleander would make a fine High King, even if he didn't belong to the high family."

"I have no objection," King Cashma said.

"I wouldn't want anyone else," King Daerwyn said.

King Redwen sighed. "Since the vote of the council is against me, it really doesn't matter what I think." His eyes flickered up toward Geniolien. "But I think somebody ought to ask Geniolien how *she* feels about all this."

"The High Princess," Geniolien said, smiling at Mole, "is happy to find a long-lost cousin and even happier," she added, glancing at Merani, "that he can take the burden of the high crown."

"There, now," Gwarthan said, beaming. "Most of the necessary votes are accounted for. But the most important vote is yet to be counted." Gwarthan turned to Mole and stated at him searchingly. "Moleander, I'm about to ask you whether you will accept the high crown. But don't answer quickly. Listen to what I say. In time you will find that both King Ellarwy and Princess Geniolien are wise in their reluctance to take the high throne. The High Kingship is no easy task; often it is an unhappy one. Wars will come, perhaps not against sorcerers but against outlaws and goblins and pretenders. Hard times will come, when you will have to suffer what the people suffer, and more, because you are their king. And it is hard and thankless work, for most often you will be condemned for what you do wrong rather than praised for what you do right. Your time will not be your own, and neither will your life. If you are to be a good High King, you will dedicate your life to others. You used to roam in the snow of Mon Ceth to find freedom, Moleander, but as High King your tastes of mountain air will be few. I want you to know what you're giving up. Think of the ash staff, Mole; once you backed away from the duty it presented. But these people aren't offering you an ash staff; they're offering you an ash tree, for which the ash staff has only been training, a tree under whose burden you will groan and weep and sweat, even when nothing seems to be going wrong. Now, knowing fully what the high crown will mean, I want you to give the council your answer."

Mole laid the ash staff in his lap. He watched colored reflections move on its polished surface. Gripping the staff, he looked up into the faces turned expectantly toward him, most of them waiting, most of them smiling. Each face seemed familiar, and the names sang through his mind: Geniolien, Ellari, Merani, Gareth, Rachim, Cashma, Eheran, Morin, Gwenith, Mair, Daerwyn. Some of the faces nearest him sparkled with joy and made silent promises with their eyes: Fflad and Arien. And beyond, perhaps in the gleam of torchlight on the windows, Mole saw more faces, dim, shrouded with time, touched with twilight and mist, but smiling at him, too: Llawer Smith, Llan, Hallwyndier, Orne, Berrian, Rhawn. All of them— and two faces more, the face of a man and woman, unfamiliar, but oddly familiar, as if from forgotten dreams—all of them watched, smiled, and waited.

Bracing himself with the staff, Mole stood up. "If you'll have me," he said, looking from face to face, "I'd like to be your king."

Dawn and the Thorn

WHEN THE LAST of friends and well-wishers had gone, Mole found himself alone in the hall, except for Arien, who waited at his side with a quiet smile. One or two of the council torches still burned, but most had gone out, leaving the hall of thrones dark except for a pale glow like moonlight on the windows. Looking across the tables toward the silent thrones, Mole suppressed a chill. All of this was his, not to have, but to care for.

"Being king will be hard, and it won't be pleasant," he said, as much to himself as to Arien. "I believe everything Gwarthan said about the problems I'll have. And I can't forget Branddabon's curse. But friends will always be a comfort, don't you think? Fflad has always given me good advice. He'll make a wonderful counselor, though I think he was more pleased with the musical side of First Friend and Minstrel to the High King. And Geniolien. She's my only living relative, you know. She'll be Queen of Pesten, and I'll rebuild my father's castle for her. Though, of course, she can stay at Drallm if she wants to. Merani can be a court lady, or an archer if she prefers."

"Merani," Arien said, "may soon be more interested in the court of Ranath Thrine than in yours. She and Crown Prince Ellari left the hall together, you know."

"But even if Geniolien goes to Ranath Caeodd and Merani to Ranath Thrine, my court will have ladies. You, of course, and Mair . . ."

Arien looked down at her hands. "Mair is much more than a lady; she is a queen. Have you ever thought what a perfect wife and mother she would make?"

Mole frowned. "No."

"You ought to notice her more, then. You're a king now, Mole, the High King, and you can't afford to cheat yourself. A king must have heirs, sons. And those sons must have a good mother—"

"Arien," Mole burst out, seizing her hands, "what are you saying? Do you think that just because I've become king I feel any different about you?"

Head bowed, Arien didn't answer.

He kissed her cheek, leaned back, then smiled at her. She smiled back, but her smile was dull, removed, and sad; her eyes seemed misted over by the seeds of tears. He lowered his eyebrows. "Tired?" he asked.

"Not really. Not too tired to go on a walk. Please."

Nodding, Mole stood up and stretched his stiff legs. He helped Arien to her feet, and together they looked over the scattered benches, then moved through the doors.

Outside dawn was near, a cold, winter dawn. Arien's hand, when Mole took it, fit loosely in his. And though he looked at her, she did not look at him. Instead she watched the sky above the east wall, scattered with faint stars like chips of ice beginning to melt. By the time they reached the castle gate, the low stars had vanished into the yellow beginnings of dawn over the mountains.

Once outside the gate, they stood together to keep from the cold. The sun's first light strayed onto the surface of the river. The rest of the castle hill remained black and cold; the burial mound was visible only because of a torch burning on its crest.

At length, Mole spoke. "Arien," he said, warming her hand between his. "Arien, I thought I'd have an easier time asking you, now that I know who my parents are, now that I'm going to be High King. But Arien, it's still hard. What I mean to say again is that Gwarthan was right. It won't be easy being High King. I can feel that already. I can't do it alone—"

"Mole," Arien said, turning from him, "please—"

"You don't have to give me an answer right now if you don't want to," Mole said quickly. "I'll wait. I'll always wait—"

"Mole," Arien said, almost fiercely, "that's not what I mean.

Listen to me. Listen to me please. Try to understand. I don't have much time."

Mole frowned. "I'm listening."

"You know that I'm a Daughter of Amreth. The third. The last."

"Of course. Your power saved me from Branddabon. You explained that."

She looked down. "Yes. But by using it, I let the fire free—oh, Mole, it's not your fault, it's not!"

"What's not my fault?"

Arien bit her lip. "That it's my time," she whispered; "that I have to go."

"Go?" Mole said. "Go where?"

Arien looked away suddenly into the brightening east. "There," she said, "into the dawn, to find Rhea and Cara and Mother Amreth and the fire that burns in the Land Beyond Dawn."

"Arien! What are you saying? I won't let you go!"

"But, Mole, it has to be! Don't you understand? *When wars and warlocks all are gone will Amreth's Daughters seek the dawn.* I don't want to leave you. I want to stay with you more than anything else in the world. But I've made my choice. I made it when I brought fire to the hall of thrones. And Mole," she said, blinking back tears, "I'm not sorry for what I did."

She shook herself away from him, but then rushed back to press a kiss to his cheek. "Mole," she said, "Mole, promise me something. I will never see you again, never, never again, not under moon or stars, not even in dreams. Promise me, promise me something now. Promise me that no matter what happens, you'll never forget me."

"Forget you?" Mole said. "Forget you! How could I ever forget you? But Arien, I won't let them take you. I'm High King now, and I won't let them!"

Quieting him with a touch of her hand on his cheek, Arien backed away. He reached after her, but she seemed to melt through his fingers. She didn't take her gaze from his, but instead of tears, her eyes filled with dawn light, fires like candles behind them. "I love you, Mole," she said; then, before he could answer, she turned away and walked toward the river. She seemed to dissolve into the dawn light, just as the shadows beneath the trees over the river faded away with the rising sun. And just when Mole could see only the last glitter of her hair, he seemed to see two shadow-women join her, then melt away with her into the golden tapestry of dawn on the high clouds.

"Arien," he said, but only in a whisper, "Arien."

But only the wind answered. Brisk with spray from the sea, it combed its way across the river and hummed in the long grass at Mole's feet. With it, from somewhere far over the river, came the faint smell of mountain flowers.

Appendix

People, Places, and Things

AEDDEN   valley in east of the Thrine: site of High King Llarandil's ancient stronghold

AEDDENON   a valley lily; symbol of High Queen Cara

AELENWAITH   island kingdom

AMMAR   first of the three sorcerers; the Dark One; ruler of Ammardon and most of Pesten for many years

AMMAR MORNG   stronghold of Ammardon

AMMARBANE   epithet for Moleander

AMMARDON   wilderness land of Ammar in northern Pesten

AMRETH   daughter of the Emperor of the North

AMRETH, DAUGHTERS OF   three enchantresses chosen by Amreth; Cara, Rhea, Arien; wielders of Amreth's flame

ARI   shortened version of Arien

ARIEN   Mon Ceth orphan; third and last daughter of Amreth

ASH TREE   symbol of the House of Llarandil

BARDS' QUARTER   school of music and poetry at Ranath Drallm

BATTLE OF AMMARDON   High King Gion's defeat of Ammar

BATTLE OF THE EAST GATE   victory of the kings' armies over the evil forces controlling Ranath Drallm

BATTLE OF NORTHMARCH   ancient victory of Strein Battle-king over the Grey Trolls

BATTLE OF RATHVIDRIAN   King Cashma's defeat of the hawk riders of Vivrandon

BATTLEKING   epithet for High King Strein

BERRIAN   crown prince of Thrinedor; a captain of Ranath Drallm

BINDING RING OF MERWNEDD   device used to determine blood relationships

BLACK COUNSELOR   second of the three sorcerers; advisor to Prince Ichodred of Vivrandon

BLACK WOOD   the Great Forest

BOOK OF GATH   volume of evil spells created before the world; most powerful instrument of black magic in the North

BRANDDABON   third and last of the three sorcerers

BRIARBORN   meaning of the name Moleander

BRIAWYN HILLS   mountain range east of Eber Ystadun

CAEODD   see RANATH CAEODD

CANDYLL-BEYOND-TARANIL   city of the Pesten coastlands

CARA   High Queen; wife of High King Llarandil; first daughter of Amreth

CASHMA   king of Sharicom

CATHYN PEAK   see MON CATHYN

CATHYN PASS   see DRAGON PASS

CELAIN   a captain of Ranath Drallm; brother of Paladain

CENDWN   one of Good Eiddew's Men

CITY OF LLARANDIL   Eber Ystadun

CLIFFTOP HOUSE   royal residence of Aelenwaith

COASTLANDS   heavily-populated sea coast between the River Thrine and Candyll-beyond-Taranil; a province of Pesten

CRAFTSMEN'S QUARTER   smithies, amories, and workshops of Ranath Drallm

CRYWYLL   kingdom west of the River Ystadun

CWYLLER   Merani's white hawk

CYRANUS   ancient poet of Pesten

DAERWYN FELLFLOOD   lord of Fellhaven; king of Vivrandon after the Battle of Rathvidrian

DAVYDD   master of Avy-Ellarwch

DARK ONE   Ammar

DARK REALM   Ammardon

DAUGHTERS OF AMRETH   see AMRETH, DAUGHTERS OF

DEHRU   father of light and life; destiny

DERWEN   Old Man of the Oak

DOLENGWRYDD   second name of High Princess Geniolien

DRAGONS OF MON CATHYN   dragons slain by High Prince Rheidol

DRAGON PASS   the path over Mon Cathyn; canyon below where High Prince Rheidol slew the dragons

DRAGONSHEAD   island in the Mouths of Ystadun; tutory of sorcerers

DRALLM see RANATH DRALLM
DRALLMBUILDER epithet for High King Gwyram

EAST GATE, BATTLE OF THE see BATTLE OF THE EAST GATE
EBER SEADOR Thrinedor coast city
EBER TARANIL city of the Pesten coastlands; second greatest city of the North
EBER YNYS chief village of Aelenwaith
EBER YSTADUN main trading city on the River Ystadun; greatest city of the North.
EHANDERAL a horse
EHERAN a captain of Ranath Drallm
EIDDEW founder and first king of Aelenwaith
EIDDEW VII king of Aelenwaith
EIDDEW NETMAKER citizen of Eber Ynys
EIDDEW THE FISHERMAN citizen of Eber Ynys
EIDDEW THE TAILOR citizen of Eber Ynys; father of Moleander Tailor
EILWICH, RING OF enchanted ring lost when High Prince Rheidol was slain; great instrument of white magic
EIREN servant of Escandrin of Aelenwaith
EITHODD fifth High King; Shipwright
ELLARI prince of Thrinedor
ELLARWCH fourth king of Thrinedor; founder of Avy-Ellarwch
ELLARWY fifth king of Thrinedor
EMNOS island home of pirates; south of Aelenwaith
EMPEROR OF THE NORTH ruler of the north
ENETOTH a senior captain of Ranath Drallm
ENNA orphan at Avy-Ellarwch
ESCANDRIN Aelenwaith lord; father of Ingradd and Ielyn
ETERU mother of light and life; eternity
EVENING MOUNTAINS the Mon Evann
EVETOTH a senior captain of Ranath Drallm

FAR PLACES where the Sword, the Book of Gath, the ring of Eilwch, and the Iron Crown of Greycrag were made
FELL DOWNS hilly country north of the River Fellflood
FELLBLOSSOM a heath flower; symbol of Rhea Lady Fellflood
FELLEIRA second name for Merani; Vivrandon family name
FELLFLOOD great river of Vivrandon; tributary of the Ystadun
FELLFLOOD Vivrandon family name
FELLFLOOD VALE fertile valley between Fellheath and the Fell Downs
FELLHAVEN town upriver from Rathvidrian

FELLHEATH   great highland of Vivrandon; moors

FELLHEATH WIZARDS   legendary northern enchanters

FENDWR   a captain of Drallm

FFLAD   orphan of Mon Ceth; harpist; poet

FIFRAN I   son of High King Llarandil; first king of Vivrandon; oracle

FIFRAN II   second king of Vivrandon

FIFRANEIRA   son of Fifran II; father of Merani

FIRE POWDER   a goblin explosive

FORRESTBOURNE   Great Forest river; tributary of the River Thrine

GARETH   Mon Ceth orphan; loremaster; prince of Sharicom

GARREN MEHRIDENE   founder of the North; maker of the Oath; first High King

GATH, BOOK OF   see BOOK OF GATH

GENIOLIEN DOLENGWYRDD   High Princess

GIEN   High Queen; wife of High King Eithodd

GION   sixth High King; Liberator

GIONSDALE   camp of High King Gion during the Battle of Ammardon

GOLDEN SHIPS   fleet built by High King Eithodd

GOOD EIDDEW'S MEN   group of Aelenwaith merrymakers

GOODBLADE   see SWORD, THE

GREAT FOREST   woodland covering most of Pesten

GREAT HEATH   see FELLHEATH

GREAT SWORD   see SWORD, THE

GREATER KINGDOMS   Pesten, Vivrandon, Thrinedor

GREY TROLLS   invaders of Pesten in the days of High King Strein; defeated at the Battle of Northmarch

GREYSTONE ROAD   Great Forest road built by High King Llarandil

GULF OF THRINEDOR   the sea off Eber Seador

GWAEL   Chief Minstrel of Ranath Drallm

GWARTHAN   white wizard; student of the Fellheath Wizards

GWENITH   daughter of Lord Morin of Ranath Drallm

GWYRAM   fourth High King; Drallmbuilder

HALLWYNDIR   knight of Eber Taranil

HARDANOG   constellation

HARDANOG DRAGONS   see DRAGONS OF MON CATHYN

HOUSE OF LLARANDIL   High King Strein and his descendants; family of the High Kings

HOUSE OF THRINEDOR   Hwyl the Good and his descendants; ruling family of Thrinedor

HOUSE OF VIVRANDON Fifran I and his descendants; ruling family of Vivrandon

HWYL THE GOOD son of High King Llarandil; first king of Thrinedor

ICHODRED prince of Vivrandon

ICHODRON third king of Vivrandon

IELYN Arien's true name

INGRA lady of Aelenwaith; mother of Ingradd and Ielyn

INGRADD Fflad's true name

IRON CROWN OF GREYCRAG instrument of black magic destroyed at the Battle of Northmarch

ISTAFEL great river of Sharicom; tributary of the Ystadun

KING OF THE GREY TROLLS leader of the invasion during High King Strein's reign; killed at the Battle of Northmarch

LAND BEYOND DAWN home of Amreth

LESSER KINGDOMS Sharicom, Crywyll, Aelenwaith

LIBERATOR epithet for High King Gion

LLAN Mon Ceth orphan

LLANDRIN Lord of Eber Seador; cousin of Escandrin

LLARAN twin of High King Eithodd; King of Pesten; High Captain

LLARANDIL THE GREAT second High King; father of kings; builder of Eber Ystadun; greatest king of his age; lawgiver

LLAWER SMITH citizen of Eber Ynys; friend of Moleander

LLONWYLON coast province of Crywyll

LORD OF THE CITY ruler of Eber Ystadun

MADDWN FELLRIDER Vivrandon outlaw

MADRIC an ancient king of Crywyll

MADRING one of Good Eiddew's Men

MAGLAW servant of Branddabon

MAIR daughter of Lord Morin of Drallm

MEADS OF CRYWYLL pasturelands west of the River Ystadun

MEDWING High Captain

MELIDOR a lord of Ranath Drallm

MERANI archer; daughter of King Ichodron's brother

MERWNEDD a Fellheath wizard

MIRA name contrived by High Princess Geniolien

MISTY MOUNTAIN see MON CETH

MOLE shortened version of Moleander

MOLEANDER   Mon Ceth orphan; bearer of the Sword; holder of the staff; Ammarbane; captain of Ranath Drallm

MOLEANDER TAILOR   son of Eiddew the Tailor

MON CATHYN   highest peak of the Mon Lluwall; site of the battle between High Prince Rheidol and the dragons

MON CETH   highest mountain of the Mon Dau; early home of Moleander and his companions

MON DAU   mountain range in eastern Pesten, running from Ranath Thrine to Candyll-beyond-Taranil

MON EVANN   mountains on the west border of Sharicom

MON GWYDD   mountains on the north border of the kingdoms

MON LLUWALL   mountains north of the Fell Downs

MON RHAW   beacon mountain; Briawyn peak east of Eber Ystadun

MORAFIN LANDMASTER   a citizen of Eber Ynys

MORIN   a lord of Ranath Drallm

MORNING MOUNTAINS   see MON DAU

MOUNTAINFLOWER   meadow flower; symbol of Arien; meaning of the name Arien

MOUTHS OF YSTADUN   where the River Ystadun meets the sea; the Ystadun delta

NIGHTBLACK   a horse

NORTH, THE   the kingdoms and the wild lands around and between; ruled by the Emperor

NORTHMARCH   forest province in northern Pesten

NORTHMARCH, BATTLE OF   see BATTLE OF NORTHMARCH

OLD MAN OF THE OAK   powerful being of the Mon Dau; Derwen

ORNE   Mon Ceth orphan

ORYGATH   the first pole star

OWAIN   orphan at Avy-Ellarwch

PALADAIN   a captain of Ranath Drallm; brother of Celain

PENEGIR   the second pole star

PESTEN   kingdom between the River Ystadun and the Mon Dau; usually ruled by the High King

PRETENDER, THE   mad outlaw of the marshes

RACHIM   crown prince of Sharicom

RANATH CAEODD   royal seat of Pesten; guardian of the Book of Gath; destroyed by goblins

RANATH CRYWYLL   royal seat of Crywyll

RANATH DRALLM   seat of the High King; fortress

RANATH THRINE   royal seat of Thrinedor; stronghold

WILD EAST PESTEN   outland province of Pesten east of the Mon
   Dau

WILDFOAL   Moleander's horse

WOLDS OF SHARICOM   sheepraising country of Sharicom

WOLDWASH   river separating Sharicom and Vivrandon; tributary
   of the Ystadun

WRATH OF THE SEA   See RETHEMOR

YNYS   see EBER YNYS

YSGARLAD   wife of King Llaran of Pesten

YSTADUN   the great river of the kingdoms; the border between
   Pesten and Crywyll; Widewater

	82630-X	**TULKU #5** *Peter Dickinson*	$2.25
	16621-0	**THE DRAGON HOARD #6** *Tanith Lee*	$2.25
	31906-8	**THE HAWKS** **OF FELLHEATH #7** *Paul R. Fisher*	$2.25
	51562-2	**THE MAGIC THREE** **OF SOLATIA #8** *Jane Yolen*	$2.25
	67630-8	**POWER OF THREE #9** *Diana Wynne Jones*	$2.25
	67918-8	**THE PRINCESS AND** **THE THORN #10** *Paul R. Fisher*	$2.25

Prices may be slightly higher in Canada.

Available at your local bookstore or return this form to:

TEMPO
Book Mailing Service
P.O. Box 690, Rockville Centre, NY 11571

Please send me the titles checked above. I enclose _____ Include 75¢ for postage
and handling if one book is ordered; 25¢ per book for two or more not to exceed
$1.75. California, Illinois, New York and Tennessee residents please add sales tax.

NAME _____

ADDRESS _____

CITY _____ STATE/ZIP _____

(allow six weeks for delivery)   T-14